The Dancing Pancake

The Dancing Pancake

EILEEN SPINELLI

ILLUSTRATED BY JOANNE LEW-VRIETHOFF

Alfred A. Knopf   New York

THIS IS A BORZOI BOOK PUBLISHED BY ALFRED A. KNOPF

Published in the United States by Alfred A. Knopf, an imprint of
Random House Children's Books, a division of Random House, Inc., New York.

Knopf, Borzoi Books, and the colophon are registered trademarks of
Random House, Inc.

Visit us on the Web! www.randomhouse.com/kids

Educators and librarians, for a variety of teaching tools, visit us at
www.randomhouse.com/teachers

Library of Congress Cataloging-in-Publication Data
Spinelli, Eileen.
The Dancing Pancake / Eileen Spinelli ; illustrated by Joanne Lew-Vriethoff.
— 1st ed.
p.   cm.
Summary: Eleven-year-old Belinda "Bindi" Winkler and her family find their
way through tough times with the love and support of the community that grows
around their newly opened restaurant, "The Dancing Pancake."
ISBN 978-0-375-85870-3 (trade)
ISBN 978-0-375-95870-0 (lib. bdg.)
ISBN 978-0-375-89713-9 (e-book)
[1. Novels in verse. 2. Family life—Fiction. 3. Restaurants—Fiction.
4. Change—Fiction.] I. Lew-Vriethoff, Joanne, ill. II. Title.
PZ7.5.S68Dan 2010
[Fic]—dc22
2009022645

The text of this book is set in 12-point Goudy.
The illustrations in this book were created using pen and ink,
then Adobe Photoshop.

Printed in the United States of America

May 2010

10 9 8 7 6 5 4 3 2 1

First Edition

To the wonderful staff and students at Glenolden School
in Pennsylvania.
—E.S.

For Max and Mattiece, my inspirations.
To Cecile and Stephanie for your enthusiasm, for your belief
in my art, and, most of all, for giving me amazing books to
illustrate. Thank you.
—J.L.-V.

Acknowledgments

A dearest thank-you to my husband and best friend, Jerry, who encouraged me to write a story to go with the title "The Dancing Pancake" when it was just a scribbled line in one of my notebooks.

To my editor, Cecile Goyette, who nudges me along with patience and wisdom.

Also to her kind assistant, Katherine Harrison.

And with fond memory of the woman in the doorway in Washington, D.C., who touched my heart, who, in my story, has become Grace.

—E.S.

A SNOW ANGEL DAY

I am on the front lawn
making snow angels
with Albert Poole.

This is what I like about Albert:
He's not afraid to do "girly" things.
He'll bake cookies as quick as
toss a football.

He'll tend the African violets
in his grandmother's front window
as tenderly as
a mama cat tends her kittens.

He likes
to shop!

What I don't like about Albert
is this: He talks about bugs
all the time.
All.
The.
Time.

He can tell you anything
        you want to know
        about horseflies or houseflies
        or dung beetles
        or cockroaches.

        And me—?
        I can tell you most anything
        you want to know about
        Albert Poole
        or classic books
        or the film *The Wizard of Oz*.

        My dad is outside, too.
        He is dumping two suitcases
        into the trunk of his car.

        I sort of hear him backing out of our driveway
        and driving off,
        but I'm not watching.
        Why should I?
        Albert Poole and I
        have snow angels to make,
        and besides, my father is simply driving to
        a different city
        to find a new job.

That's all.

That's what he said.

That's what Mom said.

That's what they both said.

C'mon, Albert!
You have to flap
your legs and arms
at the same time.

A FEW MONTHS LATER, APRIL 1ST

Mom and I are
sitting at the table
eating breakfast.
Well, I'm eating—
a crunchy blend of Cheerios, cornflakes, and
   Cocoa Puffs.
"Uh-oh," I say, pointing,
"there's a huge stain
on your blouse."
Mom jumps,
goes over to the mirror,
turns this way and that.
"Where?" she asks.
I giggle.

"April fool!"
Mom gives me a really sour look.
"Cut the jokes, Bindi,"
she says.
Huh?
This isn't like her.

TROUBLE

I am in big trouble.
My friend Megan O'Reilly
double-dog-dared me
to play an April Fool's trick
on Ms. Dee,
our principal.

It wasn't a horrible trick.
I mean, I didn't say
the school was on fire.
I just told Ms. Dee
there was a mouse floating
in the Italian dressing
on the salad bar.

Before I could add
"April fool!"
Ms. Dee went racing
for the cafeteria.
Now Mr. Stoffel,
our librarian,
just told me:
Report to Ms. Dee's office
IMMEDIATELY!

IN MS. DEE'S OFFICE

1.

I am not in big trouble.
Ms. Dee says she might even play
a trick or two
herself—later.
For now, what she wants
is for me to take
another sixth grader,
Kyra Blazak,
"under my wing."

2.

See, Kyra came to
Hamilton Middle School
in September
after being homeschooled
since she was five.
Ms. Dee says Kyra is still
having a few problems adjusting.

3.

Ms. Dee tells me that Kyra
had no homework at her homeschool.
"At home, Kyra could ask her mom
a half-dozen questions in a row."
I nod. "Kyra does ask
lots of questions in class."
"And that's fine," says Ms. Dee,
"up to a point. But sometimes
it holds up the lesson."

4.

"Another thing," says Ms. Dee.
"I notice Kyra is reading too much."
Am I hearing right? "Reading too much?"
Ms. Dee laughs. "Don't faint, Bindi.

Reading is wonderful.
But I notice Kyra reading all through lunch.
Nearly every day.
I think she could do with some company.
Some chitchat with the girls.
Can you help with all this, Bindi?"
I tell Ms. Dee I'll give Kyra a try.

5.

Ms. Dee pulls a box of candy
from her desk drawer.
She offers me a piece.
I take what looks like
a chocolate-covered caramel.
I bite into it.
It's rubber.
Ms. Dee grins.
"April fool!"

AFTER SCHOOL

After school
I invite Kyra over.
"We can do our homework
together," I say.
Kyra groans.
"I hate homework!"
"Who doesn't," I say.

Mom is in the kitchen
with my little cousin, Jackson.
Jackson is four.
Jackson is wild.
Jackson is banging on pots.
"Look, Bindi!" he hollers.
"I'm Drummer Boy!"

Mom winces.
"Drummer Boy's babysitter, Mrs. DiBruno,
had a three-thirty doctor's appointment."
"And a headache," Jackson pipes.
"From me!"

"This is Kyra, Mom," I say.
"We're going up to my room
to do homework."
"Homework!" squeals Jackson.
"I love homework!"

READING CHAIR

Kyra headed straight for the highlight
of my room—a big overstuffed chair,
yellow, with pink roses.
It almost swallowed her.
"Cool," she said.

I told her the story: My mom once worked
in a children's bookstore.
When authors came to sign
their books, they first sat in the yellow chair

and read to the people.
When the store closed down, Mom got
the chair.
Now it's my reading chair.
Sometimes I play famous writer.
I read a page from *Little Women*.
Mom claps and asks questions like
"Why didn't Jo marry the boy next door?"
Sometimes Mom pretends she's Dr. Seuss
or L. M. Montgomery. When I ask her
how rich she gets from her books
she always says, "Nunna your business, kid."

"It's a great honor," I tell Kyra,
"to be doing your homework in my reading
    chair."

AFTER MY SHOWER

Mom tells me, "Aunt Darnell came over
while you were in the shower.
She brought some of that
Italian wedding soup you like."
Aunt Darnell is a cook at Antonio's.

"And Dad called," Mom says.

I screech: "Why didn't you get me?"

Mom sighs. "You were still in that same
    shower."

"I would have come out."

"He'll call back tomorrow."

"I wanted to talk to him tonight!

I wanted to play

an April Fool's joke on him!"

"I don't think he's much in the mood

for jokes, Bindi."

I stomp off.

What's wrong with her?

Cut the jokes, Bindi.

Not in the mood

for jokes, Bindi.

Crab-crab-crab.

Jokes are what we need.

What *I* need.

INVITATION

Kyra's parents invite me
to come along
to the zoo with them
this coming Saturday.
But I have already invited
Megan to my house
to watch a movie.
Kyra's mother says,
"Bring Megan, too.
The more the merrier!"

MERRY

The Blazaks have
a big blue van.

When Megan and I
get there,
the van is practically bursting—
Kyra, little sister Krista,
Kyra's little brother Karl,
and Thet, a young man
from their church
who came from a country
called Myanmar.
He speaks very little English.
Plus Mr. Blazak's mother.
Plus Mr. and Mrs. Blazak, of course.
And now Megan and me!
Squish!

Except for a school bus
I have never been in a vehicle
with so many people.
I like it.
More *is* merrier!
I've always wanted a brother or sister—or both!
It's an old longtime wish.
And I wish that my dad will
find a job here
in *our* town
and come back home—
to *our* house—
like tomorrow.
My newest wish.

MAPS

When we get to the zoo,
Mr. Blazak gives everyone
a map of the grounds.
He assigns each of us
a site to explore:
Kyra—the bison pen,
Megan—Bird Valley,

Me—Reptile House.
Thet waves his map,
smiles,
shrugs.
Mr. Blazak puts his arm
around Thet.
"You and I will be a team,"
he tells him.
Krista, who is six, says,
"I want to be on your team, Daddy!"
Mrs. Blazak tells Krista,
"You read English, Krista.
You can find the lions
all by yourself."
Krista sighs, then studies her map.
But I understand
how she feels.
It's nice to be on a team
with your daddy.

ON OUR OWN

After lunch
Kyra and Megan and I

are free to go roaming
by ourselves.
We'll all meet
back at the elephant statue
at three o'clock.

We head to Primates.
The monkeys watch us
watching them.

As we're leaving
we hear a whistle.
The kind boys make at girls
in movies.
I say to Kyra and Megan,
"I think some boy back there
likes you."
Kyra says, "How do you know
the whistle isn't for you?"
"You think so?" I say.

There are only a few people
behind us—
parents and little kids
and an older couple.

No boys.
Hmmm . . .

Then we hear it again!
Megan's hand goes to her face.
Her eyes widen.
She points to the big monkey
with long, shaggy red hair
squatting in a tree.

"He *is* pretty cute," says Kyra.
Sure enough
he seems to be looking
straight at us.

We laugh.
We look at each other—
Hey, why not?
We walk—
well, Megan wiggles—
over to the big red monkey,
which, Kyra tells us,
is an orangutan.

We stand in front of him.
We take turns flirting.
Megan bats her eyelashes
and shimmies.
I blow kisses.
The orangutan is
nothing but bored—
until Kyra's turn.

All she does is
give a shy smile
and a wink
and the oversized monkey
starts whistling again.
We stagger away
laughing.

Back in the van
we tell
Mr. and Mrs. Blazak
all about
Kyra's new boyfriend.

DEAL

After dinner
I'm curled up on my reading chair
with *Little Women*
when Mom comes into my room
and plops onto my lap.
"Give your grumpy old mama
a hug," she says.
I give her a sly smile.
"Only if you promise to make
chocolate chip pancakes
for breakfast tomorrow."
"With pickles and seaweed on top?"
"What?"
"Just joking!"
Oh.
Mom hooks her pinkie finger
into mine. "Deal?"
"Deal."

HOUSE MOUSE

After church on Sunday
Mom and I go to
Aunt Darnell and Uncle Tim's.
Jackson squeals when he sees me
with a bag in my hand.
He is jumping up and down
on the sofa
chanting, "*House Mouse! House Mouse!*"
"Calm down," I tell him.
"I have it right here."
Jackson loves that picture book.
He wants me to read it
all the time.
I've offered to give him my copy,
or to buy him his own.
He says he only likes it when
it's my book.
I tell him he's loopy.
I don't tell him I remember
being the exact same way
myself.

Jackson snuggles against me.
I open *House Mouse* to the first page.
Jackson knows the book by heart.
He pipes: "Harry was a house mouse."
"Good job," I tell him.
"I miss Uncle Harry," he says.
My dad's name is Harry—
Uncle Harry to Jackson.
"That's not in the book," I say.
He points.
Says with force:
"Yes it is."
Something tells me not to argue.
"But you'll see him soon," I say.
"Next week. On Easter Sunday."
Aunt Darnell clears her throat.
I look up.

She and Mom have funny expressions.
Uncle Tim suddenly heads toward the kitchen.
"I'd better check the lasagna," he says.
Something queasy is happening
to my stomach.

NOT TRUE!

After we get home
Mom says
we need to talk.
She holds my hand in hers.
She says: "Bindi, honey,
your dad and I have
separated."

I can hear my heart in my ears.
"Separated?" I say. "Separated? What's
that supposed to mean?"

She rubs my hand.
She looks into my eyes.
"Bindi, you know what it means."

I pull my hand away.
I glare at her.
"That's not true!" I say. "Dad calls
almost every night. And you talk to him!
And his toolbox—what about that?
It's still in the basement.
I used his screwdriver just the other day.

"And you never even had
a big fight!
I would have heard yelling.
Why are you doing this to me?"

I jump up.
I run to my room.
I scream: "It's not true!"
Then I slam my door.
On her.
On him.
On them.

MAD-SAD-BAD

I am too . . . too something to sleep.
I kick off the covers.
I hurl my sock monkey, Ketchup,
across the room.
I toss and I turn.

In the morning my head hurts.
My stomach hurts.
I tell Mom I'm not going to school.

Mom calls me out sick.
She calls herself out
from work.

All day
we stay in our pajamas.
With the shades down.
This is true.

Mom tells me there are some things
about all this I won't understand
until I grow up.
Oh, that.
I hate when grown-ups say stuff like that.

Mom tells me part of the problem
was Dad losing his job
and getting discouraged. And moody.
And wanting time away.

"How much time?" I ask.
Mom shakes her head. "I just don't know,
   honey."
"So," I say, "Dad *will* come back
when he's had enough time away. Right?"
"Maybe. Maybe not."

I'm feeling sick. "Are you saying
you and Dad might get divorced?"
"We haven't figured things out yet."
"But you're trying, aren't you?" I say. "You're
trying to figure things out?"
"Of course we are, Bindi."

I clap my hands.
"Well, good then. Just make sure
you figure it out by Easter Sunday."
I am running off to my room
before my mother has a chance
to tell me what
an eleven-year-old-kid thing
that is to say.

HEADACHE

On Tuesday Mom goes back to work
and I have to go back to school.
Megan gives me a get-well card she made.
"Sorry you were sick yesterday, Bindi," she says.
"Just a headache," I say.
"Ginger tea can help a headache,"

Kyra tells me.
"I'll take a hundred cups, please,"
I tell her.
Mr. Stoffel says I can skip
my library-aide duties after school
if I'm still under the weather.
Albert offers to stay late
and shelve all the books himself.
I say I'm fine.
I keep an eye out for any book
about divorce.
Math Magic . . . Nonsense Poems . . .
Moby-Dick . . .
No divorce in those.

Later Albert and I walk home together.
He starts telling me about
barking spiders.
"They don't really bark," he says.
"They hiss."
He hisses in my ear. Then he says:
"If one bit you, you probably wouldn't die.
Just vomit a lot."

I tell Albert to please shut up
about barking spiders.
"Okay," he says. "So, did you know
a cockroach can live for nine days
without its head?"
I'd like to live without my head
right now.

HELP

When we get to Albert's house,
I say, "Can I come in?"
"Sure," says Albert. "Need
some help with your homework?"
"With something else," I tell him.

HUH?

See, Albert's parents are divorced.
Albert lives with his grandmother
and his dad.
I have a million questions in my still-attached
    head:
How long has it been since
his mother left?
Does he miss her?
Is he mad at her
for going away?
But before I can get all the words out,
Albert's grandmother comes in
with popcorn and juice for us.
So my one question ends up being:

"How long has it been . . .
uh . . .
since you took a bath?"
Albert's grandmother gives me
a funny look
and Albert goes, "Huh?"

OKAY

Albert and I are finally alone.
I talk in a low voice. I tell Albert
my parents may be getting a divorce.
His eyes go wide. "You're kidding!"
"Do I seem like I am?" I say.
"What happened?"
"Don't really know.
Mom says I'm too young to understand."
Albert groans. "I hate when parents say that."
I go on. "Dad lost his job. It's made him all
    moody.
Says he needs time away
from us."
I feel a sob coming on.
I swallow it.

"Maybe forever."
Albert pats my arm. "Don't worry, Bindi.
You'll be okay. Look at me.
Aren't I okay?"
I sniff. "Well,
you are obsessed with bugs."

NOT YET

I make Albert promise
not to tell anyone
about my parents'
separation.
I'm especially
not ready
to tell Megan
or Kyra.
They have such
happy,
normal
families.
I'm not ready
to admit yet
that mine

is
not.

EASTER

Dad calls and we both
cry on the phone.
Mom acts normal
but her eyes
are red and puffy.
We go to Aunt Darnell
and Uncle Tim's.
Jackson is wearing
a pink bunny suit—
my old
Halloween costume.
He hops around
all afternoon.
I want to sock him.
Uncle Tim tells
stupid elephant jokes:
"What time is it
when an elephant
sits on your fence?—

Time to get a new fence."
Ha-ha.
Time for new jokes,
Uncle Tim.
Aunt Darnell pulls Mom
into the kitchen.
They whisper
for an hour.
All I want is
to go home
and crawl under
the covers.
All I want is
for the worst Easter
of my life
to be over.

WORDS

I start hanging out more
with Albert.
Sometimes he even sits
beside me at lunch.
Megan and Kyra

look over at us
and giggle.
I know what they're thinking.
They think Albert and I
like-like each other—
like boyfriend-girlfriend.
I tell them that if I ever
do get a boyfriend
it won't be someone
who's nuts over bugs.

It will be someone
like that cute Noah Adams,
who never so much
as flicks his long eyelashes at me.
"Albert and I,
we're like brother and sister.
That's all," I tell them.
My brother.
His sister.
As soon as the words are out,
I realize how much
I love the sound of them.

KIN

Albert has just captured a spider
that was spinning a web
across my window.
He's about to bring it to his house,
let it spin a new one there.
I ask Albert:
"How would you like a sister?"
"A sister?" He puts on a think-frown.
"You mean like if my dad remarried and—"

I wave at him. "No, no. Not a real sister.
A sort of honorary sister.
Like, for instance,
me."
Albert tilts his head.
"Can people do that? Just decide?"
"Why not?"
"Will we have to live in the same house?"
"No, silly."
"Well . . ." He thinks about it way too long.
"Okay, then. I guess."
"Cool," I say. "It's settled then . . . bro."
I hold out my hand
but when he goes to shake it
I surprise him with a big
sisterly hug.
He wasn't ready for that!

AT KYRA'S HOUSE

Krista—Kyra's little sister—
is turning cartwheels
in the hallway.
She keeps crashing
into the wall.
Pictures rattle.
Krista laughs.

In one of the bedrooms,
Karl is running the vacuum.
All the Blazaks have
official chores.

Mr. Blazak is in the kitchen
helping Mrs. Blazak.
Blender whirs. Kettle whistles.
Mr. Blazak sings.

"Wow, Kyra," I say, "your house
is so noisy."
"Sorry," Kyra says.
"Oh, no," I tell her.
"I love it!"

BRAVE?

I wasn't planning
on telling Kyra
about my parents,
but she keeps asking
questions, like:
"Is your dad still away?"
"Did he find a job yet?"
"Will you be moving there?"
"Will he come home
on weekends?"
Finally I say it:
"My parents have separated."
Kyra gasps. "Oh no!"
"It's okay," I lie. "I'm adjusting."
Kyra gets all teary-eyed.
Gives me a look I've never seen before.
"You are a brave, brave girl, Bindi Winkler."
I am?

LAST

When I tell Megan
about the separation,

she gets all huffy.
"Wait a minute," she says.
"You told Albert
and Kyra
before you told
me?"
"It just happened
that way," I tell her.
"Well," she gripes,
"I guess I know now
where I stand.
Dead last."
Ouch.
I glare at her.
"Welcome to my world."
Ouch.

EAVESDROPPING

I walk in the front door.
I hear voices.
Mom and Aunt Darnell
are in the kitchen.
I tiptoe closer.
I can see a little bit of them,

I can snoop.
Aunt Darnell says, "Antonio's
is closing. I'm going to need
another job. But I don't want
just another job. I want
my own place.
Ever since I was a kid,
I've wanted my own little restaurant."
Mom says, "I remember!
All you ever wanted to play was
diner waitress or lunch truck."
Giggles.

"And you, Vera," says Aunt Darnell,
"you know darn well Harry's probably
not coming back."
How can she say that!
"You're going to
have to make a life
for yourself."
"I already have a life," Mom tells her. "I
have Bindi. And I like my job at
The Pink Lily."
That's right.
Aunt Darnell snorts: "The Pink Lily is
part-time. Low pay. You can't get by
for long on that."
Why not?
Mom says, "I'll ask for more hours.
Maybe get us an apartment. We don't
need a whole house anyway."
We don't?
Aunt Darnell beams. "Well, now
listen to this: The place I'm talking about
used to be a hamburger joint. You and I
could turn it into a cozy cafe. Just breakfast
and lunch. But the best part is, the rent
     includes

the apartment on the second floor.
Perfect for you and Bindi. You wouldn't
have to drive to work. Just skip down the
    stairs!"
Just say no, Mom. Just skip this.
After a long silence Mom says:
"Darnell, I need to think about this."
Aunt Darnell shakes her head. "There's no time
to think! Someone else will grab it."
I stomp into the kitchen.
"I'm not moving!" I tell them.
"No way!"
Not gonna happen.

DREAM

On Friday
Mom is working late at The Pink Lily.
Aunt Darnell picks me up from school.
"You can have dinner with us, kiddo,"
she says. "We'll get takeout."
Aunt Darnell parks in front of
Harvey's Hamburgers.
The place is all dark. The paint is peeling.

There is trash everywhere.
"This place is closed," I say.
Aunt Darnell pulls out a key. "My friend Karen
is the rental agent for the building.

This is the place I was telling your mom about."
Her eyes light up. She squeezes my arm.
She whispers, "This is my dream place.
You know about things like that, right?"
She tugs me inside.
Garbage smell,
greasy walls,
cracked tiles,
creepy-crawlies.
There's a dark puddle of ooze in one corner.
Dream? I say to myself.
This is one dream
we all better
wake up from
now.

PROMISE

Aunt Darnell locks the door.
We get in the car.
She turns to me.
"This is a good thing, Bindi.
It is a big chance
for all of us.

It will be hard,
but it will be fun.
You won't be sorry.
I promise!"
But I can't bring myself
to say something or anything.
I don't trust
this word "promise."
My mom and dad made a promise
the day they got married—
and look what happened.

DOES ANYONE CARE?

I ask Albert:
"Why do grown-ups even bother
to act like us kids have any say
in our lives?"
Albert is tracking a bug
across his backyard.
"Who knows," he says.
I go on: "Did anyone ask me
if Dad should leave?"
Albert keeps tracking.

"Does anyone care that
I don't want to move?"
More tracking.
"Or that I don't want any part
of this stupid restaurant?"
Turns out Albert's bug
has wings. It flies away.
Albert gives me this excited look.

"That was a box elder bug, Bindi!
They fool you.
They look like crawlies

WORK? FUN?

Megan says Aunt Darnell is right—
being part of a business can be fun.
Megan says she likes going into
the office with her parents.
She likes running the envelopes
through the stamp machine,
helping to sort the mail,
and pulling staples out of papers.
She likes taking a "coffee break"
with their secretary, Mrs. Flanders.
Especially when Mrs. Flanders
brings donuts.
Megan says if she has that much fun
in a regular old office,
think of what fun I could have
in my own restaurant.

Hmmm . . .
We'll probably have donuts
all the time.

MAY DAY

The Blazaks celebrate May Day.
The family makes up flower baskets
and Kyra hangs them on neighbors' doors
before school.
After school, Megan and Albert and I
are invited to the Blazaks' for May Day treats:
cookies iced like daisies,
strawberry shortcake,
mayapple tea.
Mr. Blazak is home from work early.
He dances Kyra and Krista around the room
singing a sweet-silly song:
"In the merry, merry month of May . . ."
Then he takes my hand—and Megan's—
and I'm dancing with Kyra's dad,
moving fast
and hoping my feelings don't show.

I CAN'T WAIT

Mr. Stoffel, our librarian, hands me
a copy of *Peter Pan*.
"A beautiful new edition, Bindi,"
he tells me, all smiles.
Mr. Stoffel is
always happy when
he hands me a book
I might like.

Megan takes the book from me
and stares at the cover.
"I thought this was a movie."
I tsk-tsk her. "It was a book first,
Miss Needs-to-Read-More."

It feels odd,
reading about someone who
does not want to grow up—
ever.
Me? I can't wait!
I can't wait to be *on my own*.
Making *my own* decisions about
whether to move.
Or whether to walk away from my family.
Or whether to go into a business.
I want to be in charge of me.
Someday.
Soon.

MAD

Guess what?
I am no longer sad about

my dad leaving.
Know why?
Because I am mad.
I turned his stupid picture
facedown in my sock drawer.
I will not take his stupid phone calls.
He just told me in his stupid e-mail
that he is so sorry about everything.
He said that when I grow up
I will understand how a person
can become "overwhelmed,"
how a person might need
a fresh start.
How he loves me.
That I'm still his Bindi-boop.
His Bindi-boop my butt.
I didn't hit "Reply."
I won't.
Ever.

SIN?

Megan says
she thinks it may be

a sin
for me to be mad
at my father.

Kyra says
mad isn't a sin.
Hate is a sin.

"So, mad is allowed?"
asks Megan.
"I think so."

Megan gives a sly grin.
"Well, I'm so mad
I could . . .
throw my math book in
the garbage disposal!"
Kyra pipes,
"I'm so mad I could steal
all my brother's underwear and—"

Suddenly I hear myself say:
"And toss them up
in the trees!"
And now we're off to

the races, imagining ourselves
doing everything
from kicking pumpkins
to screaming "Banana poop!"
in the principal's office.
We're mad,
and crazy!

CHAT

I ask Albert if
he hates his mother.
He says no.
"But aren't you mad at her?"
"Not anymore."
He offers me a gummy worm.
I pop it in my mouth.
"When did you stop being
mad at her?" I ask.
Albert squints. "I don't really know."
He shrugs,
then looks away from me.
"It just all stopped," he says.
"I woke up happy one day."

He hands me another worm.
Okay.
"Thanks, Albert."

MISERABLE

I wake up miserable.
Sore throat. Sneezing. Stuffy nose.
Mom has to go to work.
"See," she says, "if we lived
over the cafe and I worked there
I could take care of you.
I could bring you soup.
And lemon tea.
All day long.
"Achoooooo!" is my reply to that.
Then Aunt Darnell shows up with Jackson.
Jackson tromps up the stairs and
into my room.
He's wearing a stethoscope.
He tries to make his voice grown-up-low.
"Doctor Jackson will fix you up good."
He pulls a tongue depressor from

his little doctor kit.
"Open wide, sicko," he says.

BAD NEWS

After lunch
Dr. Jackson falls asleep
in the hallway,
where he had been checking
his teddy bear's heart rate.

Aunt Darnell comes into my room,
sits on my bed.
She brushes my hair. Long strokes.
It feels really good.
"You have such pretty hair, Bindi,"
she says. "I wish mine was so shiny."

I turn to her. "Your restaurant's going to
happen, isn't it?"
Her voice goes soft. "Yes, it is, kiddo."
"And Mom and I are moving?"
"Yes—when school lets out."

"I guess Mom was afraid to tell me herself."
"She was going to, Bindi."
Now my stomach hurts, too.
"Well, I don't like it."
"Can you just give it a chance?" she asks.
I flop back against my pillow.
"Can I just have a choice?" I ask.

ON MY OWN

Last year for Mother's Day,
Dad helped me choose

a plant for Mom.
Mom loves plants.
She sings to them.
This year Mom is working
for a florist, so she can get
all the plants she wants—dirt cheap.
Megan tries to help. "Fancy perfume!"
she says.
I tell her Mom doesn't wear it.
"Bubble bath?"
"She takes showers."
"Scarf?"
"She has tons."
Megan plunges on. "Hand lotion?
Earrings? Candy?"
"No, no, and no."
Megan glares at me. "Is that all you can say?
Are you sure you want to get your
mother a present?"
I glare back. "Yes."

Mr. Sourapple—Mr. Stoffel—
usually is as nice as pie.
But lately he's been
kind of snappish.

"Miss Winkler, *Peter Pan*
is three days overdue. Other people
might like to read it, you know."

And to Albert:
"Mr. Poole, if you drop
another book
you can just turn in
your library-aide button."

This afternoon Mr. Stoffel
comes to me and Albert.
"I'm sorry I've been such a bear lately,"
he says. "My neighbor's new puppy
is barking,
barking all night.
I've been sleep-deprived—
big-time!"

"That's okay, Mr. S.," says Albert,
looking right at me.
"I'm used to people
being totally crabby,
all the time."
Who, me?

SMILEY FACE

Mr. Stoffel gives us each
a smiley-face bouncy ball.
I tell Albert, "This gives me
a great idea for a Mother's Day gift."
"You're gonna give your mom
a bouncy ball?"
"Nope, dope!"
He'll see.

SMILEY CARD

Megan is a master card-maker.
She's got all kinds of neat stuff:
colored paper, ink pads, stamps,
stickers, ribbon, glitter glue.
I tell her I want to make
something happy—
something huge!

She hands me two sheets of
bright yellow paper
and these fancy scissors that
cut scalloped edges.
I draw a big smiley face.
On the front of the card
I print:
ON MOTHER'S DAY
I WILL . . .
and inside, I draw this:
☺
ALL
DAY
LONG.
Megan waggles her eyebrows,
says, "Can you do that?"

HAPPY

It's Mother's Day.
I give Mom the card.
She reads it
but she *doesn't* smile—
Oh.

She starts to cry!
"Hey, Mom," I tell her,
"I meant— It was supposed to
make you happy."
Mom blows her nose.
"It does, honey.
Sometimes the best kind of happy
comes out like this."

WHAT THE BANANA SAID

Uncle Tim takes us all out to brunch
for Mother's Day.
Uncle Tim is almost always silly.
He'd make a perfect cartoon character.
Today he acts even goofier.
Maybe he wants to keep
our minds off
the fact that
Dad isn't with us?
He twists his napkin
and plops it on his head
like horns.
"I'm Horn Head."

Jackson giggles so hard
juice sprays from his mouth.
Aunt Darnell grins at Uncle Tim.
Next, Uncle Tim does his famous
dangle-a-spoon-from-his-nose trick.
Giggle.
Finally he tells his latest elephant joke:
"What did the banana say to the elephant?"
Only Jackson replies: "Hey, don't eat me!"
Uncle Tim chuckles. He taps Jackson's nose.
"The banana doesn't say anything,
you silly-billy.
Bananas can't talk!"
And Aunt Darnell
cracks up!

WEEVIL-WICH

These days
the grown-ups
talk-talk-talk:
building codes,
regulations,
equipment,

insurance,
accounting,
advertising,
permits,
plumbing inspections.
Restaurant stuff.
Blah-blah-blah.
Now Albert's bug talk
is starting to sound
positively
fascinating.
"Did you know there is
more protein in a palm weevil
than in a BLT?"
"Great," I say,
"let's put 'em on the menu."
WLT: weevil,
lettuce, and tomato.

JOBS

The cafe will be open
for breakfast and lunch.
My aunt Darnell will cook.

My uncle Tim will handle
the businessy stuff.
My mom will do whatever else
needs doing.
They decide to open
right after school lets out.
Ruby Frances, a sixteen-year-old,
is hired for the waitress job.
She will work during the summer.
In the fall Mom will take over.
Thet applied,
with a little help from his pastor,
for the dishwasher job.
"What about me?" cries Jackson.
"I want a job, too."
Uncle Tim pats Jackson on the head.
"You can be the official litter-picker-upper."
Jackson hops up and down
like a human pogo stick.
"I'm Litter Man! I'm Litter Man!"
What will I do?
How come no one's asked me?
Do I want them to?

Less than three weeks left
of school.

As soon as school is out,
Kyra and her family
travel cross-country
in their RV.
They will visit cousins in Ohio.
Go fishing in the Snake River.
Ride horses in Oklahoma.

As soon as school is out,
Albert will go to California
to see his mother.
He'll be gone a whole month.

As soon as school is out,
Megan and her parents
fly off to Disney World
for two weeks.

As soon as school is out,
I'll be moving to an apartment

above a restaurant.
In less than three weeks.
How can I get ready
for that?

WHAT'S IN A NAME?

Mom and Aunt Darnell
are having coffee in the dining room.
They are trying to decide on a name
for their cafe.
Jackson's idea is to call it Jackson's Restaurant.
Aunt Darnell says it should be
something really catchy.
Suddenly Mom grins. "I know," she says.
She looks at me.
"Bindi, remember when
you were four years old?
How you liked
to dance your pancakes
across the kitchen table?"
"I guess so."
"Well, so, why don't we call our restaurant
dum-tah-tah-dah—

The Dancing Pancake!"
"Jackson's Dancing Pancake?"
"No, Jackson."

I HAVE TO SAY

I have to say,
The Dancing Pancake
actually looks pretty.
Even interesting,
with all the restaurant stuff—
shiny coffeemakers,
sparkling pie case,
pots so big
Jackson could
disappear into one.

I have to say,
I'm starting to think
maybe it will be
fun, being in
the restaurant business.
Did I say that?
(Not out loud.)

GOOD LUCK

Dad sends me
a four-leaf-clover key chain.
For good luck on
your final exams—
he says in his note.
I toss the key chain
into the bag
we are taking to
Goodwill.
Maybe someone else
can get lucky.

BUSY

Uncle Tim
shows up with
a small rental truck.
But not for *us*.
Mom has packed up
Dad's stuff.
Uncle Tim loads
box after box.

He will deliver
them to where
Dad lives now.
Mom says I can
go along
if I like.
I tell her I'm
really busy.
That I have lots of
painting to do.
(My toenails!)

DOWNSIZING

No way will our houseful of stuff
fit into our tiny apartment.
So we're planning a yard sale.
I ask Mom:
"If The Dancing Pancake
does really well,
could we afford
to rent a house again?
Maybe even buy one?"
She says:

"Maybe."
But for now
we have to downsize.
"Do we really need
two chairs?" asks Aunt Darnell.
She's eyeballing my reading chair.
"Don't even think about it," I tell her.

LAST DAY

On the last day of school,
Mr. Stoffel gives Albert and me
appreciation certificates
for being faithful library aides.
He gives Albert a book about
army ants.
He gives me a copy of
The Wind in the Willows.
"Keep reading!" he calls after us
as we leave the building.

As Albert and I walk together,
he tells me he's already packed
for California.

I tell him to have a good time—
and I try to mean it.
He says he will see me when he gets back.
We hug—a brother-sister kind of hug.
I head for my home
for the last time.
A rental truck is in my driveway.

MOVING

The truck is mostly loaded.
I step into my empty house.
Aunt Darnell has her arm around Mom.
When they see me
they pull me into a three-way hug.
Mom asks if I want to see my old room
one last time.
I think about it. But decide not to.
I cannot cry, I cannot cry, I cannot . . .
I go outside and wait with Aunt Darnell
and Uncle Tim, while Mom
takes one last look around.
I guess it's a good thing
we downsized. The truck

won't hold any more.
Not even a thimbleful
of memories of my dad.

MR. HELPFUL

When we pull up to
The Dancing Pancake,
Jackson runs out to greet us.
"Hi, hi, hi, everybody!"
Mrs. DiBruno has hold of his shirt.
Aunt Darnell tweaks Jackson's cheeks.
"Have you been a good boy for
Mrs. DiBruno?"
Jackson doesn't answer.
Mrs. DiBruno gives a feeble smile.
"He tried."
Then Mrs. DiBruno leaves and
Jackson scrambles up the ramp
and into the truck.
He tugs at a box twice his size.
Uncle Tim says, "That one's too big
for you, buddy."
"I can do it!" Jackson squeals

just before he and the box
go crashing.

CROWDED

I head straight for my new room,
whose walls are still slime green.
Uncle Tim hammers my bed together.
Aunt Darnell makes it up.
Then she and Uncle Tim
bring in my bureau
and my small computer table.
Already it feels too crowded.
Suddenly it hits me:
There's no room for my reading chair!
I want to—to—
to say a bad word.
I will!
I do.
Jackson wags his finger at me.
"No potty-talk, Bindi," he says.
I'm ready to bop him.
Uncle Tim gives me a weird look,
scoops up Jackson,

and hauls him back out to the truck.
And I sit on my bed and
I'm crying, crying, crying.
Because I have to.

DOWN THE HALL

Why doesn't Mom come in
to comfort me?
Why doesn't Aunt Darnell come in
to comfort me?
I hear a sound coming
from down the hall.
I stop crying.
I blow my nose.
I listen
to someone else
crying.
It's Mom.
Gee.

Things are in place—
most things.
My reading chair
is in a corner of the living room.
But it's still a great chair.
We put a good lamp
next to it.
We stare at all the boxes still waiting to be
    unpacked.
Aunt Darnell yawns and says,
"Tomorrow is another day."
She and Uncle Tim and Jackson leave.
Mom's eyes are still red.
She pets her plants. Whispers:
"Welcome to your new home,"
to the ivy.
"Everything will be fine,"
to the fern.
"It will be,"
I say to her.
But will it?

AFTER MIDNIGHT

It's late.
Mom kisses me good night.
I go to my room,
get into my pajamas.
I look
out my bedroom window:
neon signs,
clattering trucks,
yowling cat.
There's a faint scent
in the air. Burning rubber?
Not a tree in sight.
I pull down the shade.
Turn out the light.
Sit on the edge of the bed
in the dark.
I pet my own head.
I whisper:
"Everything will be fine."

BETTER

I read somewhere
that things often
seem better in the morning.
And this morning they do.
I wake up to the smell of
sizzling bacon.
To the sound of
Mom humming.
To the sight of
my Reading Hippo poster
smiling down at me.
Mom must have taped it up
in the middle of the night
while I was sleeping.
That's better.

AFTER BREAKFAST

Mom goes down to
The Dancing Pancake
to help Aunt Darnell
and Uncle Tim

get the place ready
for Monday's Grand Opening.
Uncle Tim has taken
a couple weeks'
vacation time from his job.
"Once the restaurant
is up and running," he says,
"your mom and your aunt Darnell
should be fine.
It's only a small place."
Mom says I can
come down and help.
If I want.
Do I want?

MISS MOLE

I get busy.
I make my bed
and mop the floor.
I hang two more posters.
I put underwear and socks
in the second-to-the-top drawer
of my bureau.

Games go in the closet.
My books go on the shelves.
The last book I take
from the carton is
Mr. Stoffel's gift:
The Wind in the Willows.
I bring it to my chair
and begin to read:
"The mole had been working very hard all
    morning. . . ."
I smile.
A real smile.
You can call me Miss Mole!

EAGLES

On Sunday
we all go to church.
Before the sermon starts
Jackson and I leave
for Sunday school.
Jackson is in "Sparrow Class."
He has to flap his arms
like wings

down the hall.
I am an "eagle."
Albert is an eagle, too.
But today he is soaring off
to California.
I miss my eagle-brother.

WELL-WISHERS

After church
Jackson goes to
Cole's house
to play with
his friend and fellow sparrow.
The rest of us
go back to The Dancing Pancake.
An RV
is parked in the alley
behind our building.
It is the Blazaks'!
Kyra!
Mr. Blazak says
they are getting a late start
on their cross-country trip.

Mrs. Blazak says they wanted
to wish us well with
our Grand Opening tomorrow.
She hands Mom a bouquet of sunflowers.
Kyra gives me a card that
she and Megan made together.
It reads:
We hope you will be happy
in your new home.
We will be back soon
to decorate
your new room.
You can pay us
in French fries.
I feel a sob coming on—
a happy sob—
but a sad one, too.
Why didn't I make a have-a-good-trip
card for them?
Or for Albert?
I always used to do stuff
like that.

GRAND?

Grand Opening!
The Dancing Pancake is
open for business!

A fly dive-bombs
into Aunt Darnell's
pancake batter.
Grand splash!

Jackson
"accidentally" flushes
one of his Spider-Man socks
down the toilet.
Grand whoosh!

Mom's blue hair clip
falls into the coffee urn.
Grand plunk!

Ruby Frances,
the waitress
Mom hired,
oversleeps.
Grand zzz . . .

We only get
a handful
of customers.
Grand sigh.

One is a Dr. Bingo,
who says he can't
pay today
because he forgot
his wallet.
Grand boo-boo.

Welcome to
the not-so-grand opening
of The Dancing Pancake.

GENIUS

"We need a plan," says Mom,
"fast."
"Something to get people in here,"
says Aunt Darnell.
"So they can see what a great little place
this is," says Uncle Tim.
"I know," pipes Jackson. "Free food!"

I tell Jackson, "This is a business.
We need to make money."
But Aunt Darnell is smiling.
"Maybe your cousin is onto something."
She snaps her fingers,
points at my mom.
"Free pancakes—
one day only.
What a great gimmick!"
She holds out her arms to Jackson.
"Come here, my little genius."
After closing time Uncle Tim
puts up a big sign in the window:
DELICIOUS PANCAKES!
FREE!
ALL YOU CAN EAT!!!
COME TO OUR
NEW GRAND OPENING!

PANCAKES LIKE CRAZY

Everyone flips for our pancakes.
The line into The Dancing Pancake
curls all the way around the block.
Mom helps Ruby Frances wait tables.
Uncle Tim takes over the counter,
keeps the coffeemakers bubbling.
Thet is elbow-deep in dirty dishes.
Aunt Darnell flips pancakes like crazy.
I fill endless syrup bottles,
napkin holders, sugar jars.
Jackson— who was supposed to be
quietly coloring at the counter--
starts "decorating" the menus.
We are busy and whizzy
and spinning through the day.
It's so tiring!
And . . . fun?

FLAT PANCAKES

No more free pancakes
equals only seven customers.
"All businesses start slow,"
says the last customer,
Mike the mechanic.
"Things will pick up."
In my life?

DELIVERY

Just before Mom locks the door,
a man arrives with a plant.
"Delivery for Vera Winkler,"
he says.
Mom sets the plant on the counter.
The tag says "Peace Lily."
The card reads:
May the pancakes dance off the plates—
Love, Harry
Mom strokes the leaves.
"Hi, you pretty thing."
Peace lilies must be strong.

Considering the look
coming from Aunt Darnell,
I'm surprised this one doesn't
drop dead on the spot!

PEACE LILY

I look up
"peace lily"
in Mom's
plant encyclopedia.
Here is what
it says:
The Latin name is
Spathiphyllum lynise.
The peace lily
thrives
in the deep shade
of the tropical
rain forest.
It consumes
a lot of water.
It is not affected
by insects.

If the peace lily
stops flowering,
just be patient.
It will bloom
again.
Did Dad choose
a peace lily because
he and Mom are
at war?

BREATHLESS

When I tell Ruby Frances
I like how she does her hair—
a different style every day—
she says she will do mine too.
After closing
we go up to the apartment,
into the kitchen,
where there is a sink,
a straight-back chair,
and enough room.
She tells me
she thinks Thet is adorable.

She pats her heart. "If only
he spoke more English."
I tell her my parents
are separated.
She says she already knew.
She says she hopes
I'm not holding my breath
waiting for them
to get back together.
She says most married people
who split up
never get back together.
She says, "It's just statistics."
I exhale, loudly.
I tell her,
"I'm not holding my breath."

AGAIN

I finished *The Wind in the Willows*.
Now I'm reading *The Yearling*.
It's the middle of Chapter 12.
I stop.
There's all this stuff about the kid

and his father
hanging out together.
I keep coming to lines like
"Move close, son, I'll warm you."
I start to cry.
Again.
I guess I'm not
as finished with *sad*
as I thought.
I wish I was still
just mad.

TIME

Mom says it's time for a chat.
She pours lemon tea,
which means this chat is serious.
"Sunday is Father's Day," she says.
"Your dad would like to see you."
"I don't want to see him," I say.
Mom's eyebrows get very pointy.
"It's been nearly three months, Bindi."
"So?"
"So maybe it's time to cut him a break."

I shrug. "He's the one who left."
"He's still your dad."
"He's not coming back," I say.
I tell her, "It's statistics."
Mom sets her mug of tea down.
"This is not about
Dad coming back
or not coming back.
We don't know
what's going to happen.
This is about Father's Day."
I run my finger around the rim of my mug.
Twice.
"I'll send him an e-mail.
A short one."
Mom nods, smiles, pats my hand.
"Don't get all excited," I warn her.
"I'm still mad, *just like you*."
I bet.

PROMISES

This morning's Sunday school
lesson is about

promises.
How God keeps His—
so we should keep ours.

I wish I could forget
that I told Mom
I'd send Dad an e-mail
on Father's Day.
Next time
I'll be more careful
about what
I promise.
Promise.

TO H.S.WINKLER@TEL.2.COM

*Happy Father's Day
from Belinda Winkler,
your daughter.*
I press "Send."
Kept my promise.
Done.

CASTLE

Jackson and I watch
a TV show about castles.
He gets all excited.
He says he's going to buy one
for our entire family.
"You can live in it, too, Bindi!"
"Castles cost a lot," I tell him.
"Where will you get the money?"
"I'll make Mommy give me
a better job. Not just that dumb
litter-picker-upper job.
I'll save all my pay."

FEELING GOOD

I help Jackson make
a bank out of
a milk carton.
I drop four quarters in it.
Jackson hugs my legs.
"You are my best cousin, Bindi!"
It seems like a long time

since I made anyone happy.
I almost forgot
how it feels.
(FYI: It feels terrific.)

CASHIER

The next afternoon
Jackson drags a wooden crate
over to the cash register.
He climbs on top.
"Look, Mommy," he calls,
"I can work the cash register.
I can do a good job."
"Don't you touch
that cash register!"
Aunt Darnell says.
"I can do it!" yells Jackson.
Uncle Tim scoops Jackson
into his arms. "Listen to your mommy, buddy."
Jackson whines. "I need a real job,
I want to buy a castle."
Ruby Frances slips off her shoes.
"I'll give you fifty cents

to rub my sore feet."
"Eeewwww!" cries Jackson.
"Put those stinky feet away!"
"Okay, but no fifty cents for you."
"Oh," says Jackson.
Then: "I'll rub just one foot."

MAIL

I get a postcard
with a picture of a cardinal
and a red carnation
(Ohio state bird and flower)
from Kyra.

I get a sale flyer
from Burke's Book Store.
I mark two books
I may want to
check out.

I get a package
from my father.
It's a small music box

with a rainbow
painted on the lid.

When I open it
it plays
"Somewhere over the Rainbow"
from *The Wizard of Oz*.
Geez.
Dad and I watched that movie
a dozen times.
I can feel myself
starting to get . . .
Geez.

I close the lid.
I stuff the music box
into somewhere . . .
the back of my closet.

NEW CUSTOMER

Our newest customer
wears a curly brown wig,
a man's gray sweater,

and ratty red high-tops.
One lens of her glasses
is cracked.
At least one tooth
is missing.

She pulls a rickety cart
stuffed with clothes,
newspapers,
a blanket.
She comes in most every day.
Always orders the same thing:
"Coffee, toast . . . and
extra jelly, waitress-girl."

Aunt Darnell always adds
something extra to her plate—
a slice of ham . . . a fried egg . . .
a blueberry pancake.
She tells the lady they are mistakes.
She tells the lady to just pay for
the coffee and toast.

One day Jackson goes over
to her table. "I'm Jackson,"

he says. "What's your name?"
"I'm Grace," says the lady.
"Can you get me more jelly?"
"Will you give me a tip?"
says Jackson.
"I'm buying a castle."

WHAT IS HOMELESS?

Mrs. DiBruno is off visiting her son
in South Carolina.
On Sunday, Mom and I babysit Jackson
so Aunt Darnell and Uncle Tim
can go to the movies.
I've been asking Mom questions about
Grace and homelessness.
"What's 'homeless'?" asks Jackson.

"It means having no place to live," I tell him.
Jackson's eyes go wide. "Where does Grace
    sleep?"
"Maybe in a shelter," says Mom.
"What's a shelter?" asks Jackson.
Mom tells him, "It's a place where people
who are homeless can get out of bad weather.
Or rest. Or take a shower."
We don't tell Jackson that some homeless
    people
sleep in doorways or on park benches.
Jackson folds his arms across his chest. "I'm
inviting Grace to move into our castle!"

That night I lie awake in my bed.
My room is not the best.
But I have a room—
with books on the shelves
and posters on the wall
and a place for my clothes.
I don't have to
pull my stuff around
in a cart all day
and sleep in scary places
at night.

Jackson's list
of castle-mates
is getting longer and longer.
Besides Mom and me
("and Uncle Harry, too,"
he declares),
there's his friend Cole
and the entire class of "sparrows."
He's invited my friends—
Albert, Megan, and Kyra.
Ruby Frances.
Thet.
And now Grace.
"You're going to need
a really big castle,"
I tell him.
Jackson waves
the milk carton bank
in my face.
"More donations, please."

EXCITEMENT

Megan is back from
Disney World!
Her mom drops her off
to spend the day at
The Dancing Pancake.
Ruby Frances is showing off
the tiny butterfly tattoo
on her shoulder.
Thet is singing a Burmese song.
One of the customers
is doing magic tricks for Jackson—
pulling quarters from
his nose.
Aunt Darnell fixes Megan and me
waffles with strawberries
and whipped cream.
We sit in the back booth.
Megan sighs. "You are so lucky,
Bindi. Your life is ten times
more interesting than mine."
I look up from my waffle.
"Are you kidding? You just
got back from Disney World."

104

"Yeah," she says. "But I don't *live*
in Disney World."
Then she squeals, points out the window.
"Look, Bindi, there's a policeman.
He's arresting somebody right outside.
You're *so* lucky."

WHAT?

The policeman
walks into
The Dancing Pancake.
He nods at Mom.
"Officer Pike, ma'am.
You the owner here?"
"One of them," she says.
"Well, I have your father
in my car."
Mom's jaw drops. "Huh?"

WEIRD

My grandfather Harcum died
two years before I was born.

Aunt Darnell runs out of
the kitchen
with a spatula still in her hand.
"What's going on?" she asks.
Megan and I leave our waffles
to move closer to the action.
Mom stays calm. "Officer Pike," she says,
"I can tell you for sure, whoever is in
your car is not our father."
Megan pokes me, whispers: "See?
It's like a TV show
around here."

MISTAKEN IDENTITY

The man in Officer Pike's car
is Dr. Bingo.
This is what seems to have happened:
Dr. Bingo stepped out
of the apartment building
where he lives—
to get the newspaper.
He forgot his key.
He was wearing pajamas
without shoes.

But he had been to the restaurant
and he remembered Mom's good coffee
and Aunt Darnell's French toast.
So he started walking to
The Dancing Pancake.
Officer Pike stopped to ask Dr. Bingo
where he lived.
Dr. Bingo could not remember
his exact address or his phone number.
Maybe he got nervous
because of the policeman.
Who knows?
So he told Officer Pike
he lives at
The Dancing Pancake.
With his daughters
and granddaughter.

NEW HELPER

Jackson plops down in the booth with Megan
    and me.
Now we're drinking milk shakes.
"Is Dr. Bingo going to jail?" asks Jackson.

"No," I tell him. "Officer Pike will find out
where Dr. Bingo lives and bring him home."
"I know where I live," says Jackson,
"and I'm only four and a half."
"You're smart!" says Megan.
"I'm going to invite Dr. Bingo to
live in my castle," says Jackson.
I remember what Kyra's mom said.
"The more the merrier," I tell Jackson.
I ask Megan if she wants to head up to
    my room.
She says not yet. She asks if she can
wipe the counter and clean the pie case.
"I get your tips," says Jackson.

NEVER AGAIN

Last year, on the Fourth of July,
we all went to the shore.
I love how the sun shimmers
on the sand like glitter glue.
I love the beachy blue sky.
I love the sound of the waves.
This year Mom says we can't afford to go.

Every extra penny has to go into
The Dancing Pancake.
I understand. It's just . . .
I love the beach.

GET USED TO IT

Ruby Frances and I
have become close.
She's like an older cousin to me.
She says I can come to her
with any problem.
Especially boy problems.
She says she's an expert on those.
I tell her the only boy in my life
other than Jackson
is Albert.
"Have you ever kissed Albert?" she asks.

"No!" I screech. "Never!"

"Ever want to?"

"No!" I screech. "Never!"

Ruby Frances giggles. "I wouldn't mind kissing Thet."

I slap her arm. "You'll scare him to death."

Then she says: "I saw Mike the mechanic flirting with your mother."

"You did not!" I say.

"Did too," she says. "You'd better get used to it, Bindi. Your mom is practically single now."

Is she?

FOURTH OF JULY

I let Jackson splash me.
I laugh at Uncle Tim's newest joke.
I beat Aunt Darnell at badminton.

As Mom and I leave the fireworks
that night
I remind her
that she's still married.
"I know that," she says, and smiles.
"Yeah," I say. "But does
Mike the mechanic know it?"
"Oh, Bindi," she says.
What does that mean?

DANCE

Mom sends Ruby Frances and me
to the bank for pennies.
Along the way we see Dr. Bingo
and a lady with gray hair
arguing on the sidewalk.
The lady is holding

a pair of men's shoes.
Dr. Bingo is barefoot.

When he sees me and Ruby Frances,
he grins. "Hey," he says. "It's the
pancake girls!"
The lady turns. "I'm Mrs. Coleman,"
she tells us. "Dr. Bingo's landlady.
He's refusing to wear his shoes.
Again."

Ruby Frances drapes her arm
around Dr. Bingo.
"You can't dance on this street
without shoes, Doc."

Dr. Bingo's eyes brighten.
"Dance?"
He sits on the curb.
He puts on his shoes
and starts to dance.

Ruby Frances joins him.
Then she pulls me
into the dance, too.
I remember how
Dad and I danced
one winter
under lamplight
in the snow.
He twirled me round and round
till I got dizzy
and fell over laughing.
He called it the Bindi Boogie.

It's Albert's turn
for the grand tour of
The Dancing Pancake.
He said he had a good visit
with his mother
but he's glad to be home.

Like Megan,
Albert thinks
it's really cool
to be part of a restaurant.
Thet lets Albert have a turn
at being the dishwasher.
He loses control of the spray nozzle!
Ruby Frances lets him
bring extra butter
to one of the tables.

Albert meets Dr. Bingo
and Mrs. Coleman,
Grace and Officer Pike.
I point out Mike the mechanic.
I tell Albert I am

keeping an eye on Mike.
I tell him I don't like
the way he flirts with my mom.
Albert asks why it bothers me
so much.
"Are you expecting your dad
to come back?" he asks.
Oh.
Am I?

INKY

Jackson uses fifty cents from
his milk carton bank
to buy a fuzzy fake spider from
one of those gumball machines
at Kmart.
He names the spider Inky.
He keeps Inky in his pocket
when he is not placing it
on a napkin holder
or in the pie case
or waggling it in front of
Ruby Frances, who screams

every time.
Not me.
Albert has taught me
which ones to steer clear of.

COMPLAINER

"Do you have pickled eggs?"
asks a customer
whose wrists jingle
with silver bracelets.
Ruby Frances calls out
to Aunt Darnell:
"Do we have pickled eggs?"
"No, sorry," calls Aunt Darnell.
The customer snorts,
opens a menu.
Jingle-jingle.
She decides on two eggs:
"Over easy,
lightly,
lightly." And:
"Rye toast—no butter.
Coffee—only if it's fresh-made.

Orange juice—only if
there's no pulp."
Jingle-jingle.
Ruby Frances writes
everything down.
Five minutes later
she serves the
Jingle Lady.
The Jingle Lady
jabs at
one of the yolks
with her fork.
"You call this
over easy?" she snarls.
Jingle-jingle.

GIMMICK

The Dancing Pancake
seems to have a steady group
of regulars now.
But Aunt Darnell says
a business must keep
attracting new customers.

"We need another gimmick,"
she says. "Something clever.
Something that'll grab people's attention."
"Like Inky?" asks Jackson.

UNIQUE

A couple days later
Aunt Darnell comes in
grinning.
She hands me a big bag.
"This should bring us
new customers," she says.
I pull the thing out of the bag.
It's flat and round
and golden brown.
"What is it?" I ask.
Aunt Darnell goes
all bird-chirpy.
"It's a pancake costume.
See? Armholes.
Eyeholes."
I'm shocked.
"You're going to wear

a pancake costume?"
I ask.
Aunt Darnell gives me
a crooked smile.
"No, dear niece, not I . . ."

NO WAY

Mom and Aunt Darnell can
beg,
threaten,
or pay me a million dollars,
but no way
am I ever—
ever!—
going to stand outside
The Dancing Pancake
wearing that—that—
thing!
It's stupid.
It's embarrassing.
It's totally uncool.
No way.
E-V-E-R!

(Well, I would
for a million.
But that's not gonna happen!)

BABY

I was born in Oklahoma.

Kyra sends me
a picture of herself
in Oklahoma
standing beside
the world's largest peanut.
Grace, sitting at her usual table,
overhears me telling Ruby Frances about it.
She calls me over.
"I was born in Oklahoma," she says.
"Oklahoma City."
I try to picture Grace—
homeless Grace—as a baby.
I can't.
And yet I know she must have been
a baby once.
A pink bundle,
cooing and crying,
splashing and napping.

Maybe even shaking her feisty little fist
at the tough old world.
So,
what happened?

LIKING MIKE

It's raining.
The apartment is
shadowy.
Mom is ironing her blue skirt
and some blouses.
She likes me to read to her
while she irons.
Tonight she says she's in the mood
for poetry.
"Okeydokey," I rhyme.
I find a couple of poems
about rain.
She reminds me that
when I was little
I thought rain meant
angels were crying.
When I finish the second poem

I close the book.
I ask Mom the question
that has been bothering me:
"Do you like Mike?"
Mom sets the iron down.
"Mike from the auto shop?" she says.
"Yes."
"Sure," she tells me. "He's a nice man.
A good customer."
I give her a look. "That's not the kind
of like I'm talking about."
"Ahhh," says Mom. "You mean
the kind of like where he and I
will fly off to some tropical island
together—"
"Mom!" I screech. "I'm serious!"
She plops on the sofa. "Sorry, honey.
The answer is no. I don't
like Mike 'that way.'
I love your father."
I'm—I'm— "You do?"

INFO

Mom pats the sofa.
I sit down, lean against her.
"Really?" I say. "You still
love Dad?"
She nods. "Really."
"Even though he moved out?"
"Even though."
"But you're mad at him.
I know you are.
I saw that silly T-shirt he gave you
all cut up and in the ragbag."
Mom takes a deep breath.
"Well, all I can say is, a person
can be mad—and love somebody
at the same time."
I don't want Mom to get hurt.
I don't want her to get her hopes up.
I remind Mom of Ruby's "statistics":
"People who separate almost never
get back together."
"Thanks for the info," Mom says,
"but there are always exceptions
to 'almost never.'"

Albert says
one thing he has learned
from his study of insects
is that strange, unpredictable things
happen constantly.
"Take the coffin fly, for instance.
It can live almost anywhere:
from a buried coffin, to a fungus, to a flower.
Sometimes millions share
the same coffin—
giving birth to a new generation
every few weeks—for years
and years, without ever encountering
sunlight or fresh air."

I see what Albert means—
about new life growing out of
things that seem useless
or dead.
But I'll take my old house
over a coffin,
any day.

BIG WORDS

Megan and I
are in the back booth.
Jackson wants to play Scrabble with us.
"You can't," I tell him. "You
don't know how to spell words."
"Yes I do!" he protests.
"C-a-t. Cat!
M-a-t. Mat!
M-o-m. Mom!"
He sticks his tongue out at me.
"See?"
"Forget it," I tell him. "You
need to spell big words."
"I can!" he wails.
I remain calm. "You can't."
"I can."
"You can't."
Just then Mrs. Coleman comes in.
She says, "Why don't you kids
go visit Dr. Bingo?
He's feeling lonely today."
Jackson tugs at my sleeve. "B-i-n-g-o.
Let's go, Bindi. Let's go visit Dr. Bingo."

Dr. Bingo's real daughter lives in Seattle.
I think Dr. Bingo doesn't get much company.
When he sees us at the door
of his apartment,
he does a little spin—
a slow, old man–type spin.
Dr. Bingo says he used to be
a country doctor.
He says he used to take
eggs and blueberries for payment.
But Mrs. Coleman already told me
the true story, that Dr. Bingo
only worked for a doctor—
doing landscaping and carpentry.
When the real doctor retired,
he gave Dr. Bingo one of his black bags.
And a stethoscope.
And a skeleton named Witherspoon.
I'm not sure why Dr. (Mr.?) Bingo
thinks he's a doctor.
But I don't think he's exactly lying.
Dr. Bingo opens the coat closet.
"Say hello to Witherspoon," he says.

I salute. "Hello, Witherspoon."
Jackson taps Witherspoon's hand,
squeals.
Megan doesn't look right.
She starts to wobble.

TOO MUCH

Mrs. Coleman comes in, slams the closet
    door shut.
Megan is lying on Dr. Bingo's sofa.
Dr. Bingo is rummaging through his black
    doctor bag.
"Now where the heck did I put my stethoscope?"

Mrs. Coleman lifts Megan's head.
"Take a sip of water, dear."
Jackson pats Megan's shoulder.
"Don't be scared," he tells her.
"Witherspoon won't hurt you. He's completely
    dead."

I say, "Geez Louise, Megan.
I thought you *liked* interesting stuff."

WILL WORK FOR CASTLE MONEY

Jackson is desperate for jobs.
He says there's hardly
any money in his bank
for the castle.
He begs our customers:
"I need a job. Can you give me one?"

Officer Pike offers to pay Jackson
to keep an eye on his car
while he eats his lunch.
Jackson drags a wooden crate
out to the sidewalk and sits by the car.
"I'm practically a police," he tells passersby.

Dr. Bingo "commissions" Jackson to draw
a portrait of himself to send to
his daughter.

Mrs. Coleman hires Jackson
to put stamps on her bill envelopes
while she drinks her coffee.

Mike the mechanic gives Jackson
a pocketful of change
to pass out his business cards.

Jackson's bank starts to fill up.
He tells me he thinks he'll
have enough to buy our castle
soon.

I give him a thumbs-up
and wonder:
Was I that optimistic when I was
four and a half?

"A robber stole my Inky!"
wails Jackson.
"Good!" says Ruby Frances.

"What kind of a robber
would want that creepy old thing?"
asks Aunt Darnell.

Mom says, "Bindi, help
Jackson find his Inky."
I check under the tables.
I look in the cubby where
we keep aprons
and in the corner where
we keep brooms.

"Inky's robbed!" Jackson tells Grace.
Grace starts looking, too.
She points. "There it is, sonny.
On top of that donut."

Ruby Frances screams.
Thet comes racing

out of the kitchen.
He and Ruby Frances
crash into each other.

The next morning Thet has
his arm in a sling.
Inky is barred from
The Dancing Pancake
forever.

LIVING ROOM

Someone has dumped an old green sofa
in the back alley.
It's gushing its stuffing.
Grace is sitting there, legs poking out
from her faded skirt,
one high-top sneaker dangling off,
like it's the living room of the home
she doesn't have.
But the big shocker is this:
She's reading a newspaper!

SO?

I tell Ruby Frances,
"Grace reads the newspaper."
Ruby Frances shrugs. "So?"
"*Homeless* Grace?"
"So?"
"So—I didn't know
homeless people
read newspapers."
"You are such a kid, Bindi,"
says Ruby "Old Lady" Frances.
"Of course homeless people
read newspapers.
Just because she doesn't
have a home
doesn't mean she doesn't
have interests. Doesn't
mean she's not part of
the world. Doesn't
mean she can't be
an informed citizen."

JACKSON TATTLES

Jackson sees Mom take
twenty dollars
from the cash register
and put it in her pocket.
He yells: "Mommy!
Aunt Vera is stealing!"
Aunt Darnell explains:
"No, pumpkin, the cash register
owes that to Aunt Vera."
" 'Cause she works here?"
"Yes."
"That's good," says Jackson.
"Then Officer Pike won't have to
put her in jail."

NEW DRIVER

Ruby Frances got her driver's license.
She's so happy. Like a little kid.
She twirls around The Dancing Pancake.
Sings that old Beach Boys song
"I Get Around" ("Round round get around . . .").

She asks Jackson, "Where do you want to go?"
He shouts: "To Disney World!"
Ruby Frances laughs. "Well, I can't drive
    that far."
"How come?" Jackson asks.
"I need more experience," she tells him. "Plus
I don't have my own car yet. I'm driving my
mother's car."
"You need to save up. Like me," Jackson
    tells her.
"So you can buy a big car and take me in it."
He runs off. He comes back with an empty milk
    carton.
"I can show you how to make this into a bank."

In six years I will learn to drive.
First stop: Concord, Massachusetts—
Louisa May Alcott's Orchard House, where
she wrote *Little Women*.
I'll drive everywhere—
everywhere but a certain place
where a certain person who
left his family lives.

CHAT WITH GRACE

Grace is out back
sitting on that old sofa
reading her newspaper.
I walk over.
"Hi, girlie," she says.
"Hi, Grace. What's in the news?"
Grace frowns. "Mostly bad stuff.
I like the good news.
Babies born.
Engagements.
Wedding photos."
I've been wondering
if Grace was
ever married.
I ask her.
"No," she says. "I never
met Mr. Right."
I tell her: "My mom
thought she
met Mr. Right—my dad.
Now they're separated."
Grace pats my hand.
"I'm sorry. Sometimes, girlie,

life is just plain hard."
I think about
how hard it must be
to be homeless.
But I don't say that.
Grace brightens.
"But, girlie," she tells me,
"sometimes life is just plain
wonderful.
Did you see that
sunrise
this morning?
It was a wing-dang-doodle!"
I think this means
it was pretty.

JUST TO THE PARK

Ruby Frances begs Mom,
"Just to the park, Mrs. Winkler,
pleeeeeeze."
Ruby Frances has her mother's car today.
She wants to drive me just to Halley Park.
Four blocks down Two Street, turn left,

two more blocks to the park.

"Me too!" cries Jackson.

"No," says Aunt Darnell. "Ruby Frances needs more driving experience."

"She has a lot!" cries Jackson.

Ruby Frances pats Jackson on the head. "This is just girls today."

"Boogerheads!" says Jackson.

"No potty-mouth," says Aunt Darnell.

Mom finally says I can go.

But there are conditions.

"No farther than Halley Park."

We agree.

"Bindi, you're in the backseat."

"How come?" I ask.

"Safer there," says Mom.

"And seat belts on, girls."

Of course.

"No radio. No cell phones. No texting. No distractions."

"Can do."

"And if it starts to rain—"

"Mom," I wail. "Let it go!"

It seems funny—sitting in the backseat
while Ruby Frances drives.
Like I've hired a limo.
Mom says the passenger-seat air bag
could hurt me worse than a crash
because I'm small.
I don't like being called small.
Jackson is small.
I'm eleven. I'm practically a teenager.
Then Mom says:
"Ruby Frances, please remember
you are carrying precious cargo."
I don't like being called
precious cargo, either.
Or do I?

MELTING

Ruby Frances parks the car.
We buy ice cream cones,
sit on a park bench,
and lick and talk.

Mmm . . . de-lish.
Some boys are playing basketball.
I see Noah Adams from school.
I point him out.
Albert doesn't like Noah,
he says he's stuck on himself.
But I think he's cute.
Mmm . . . de-lish.
I like how he clowns around
in class sometimes.
Even the teachers think he's funny.
Ruby Frances grins. "Aha! You
have a crush."
"Yeah," I say. "But don't worry.
Noah has never said one word to me.
Not even 'hey'!"
Hmmm . . . maybe soon?

HEY

Ruby Frances
says to hurry up with my ice cream—
we have to get back.
All of a sudden

a basketball comes
dolloping our way
and knocks my ice cream cone
out of my hand and onto the grass.
Noah Adams runs over.
"Hey," he says. "That's our ball."
Hey, he talked to me!

PACKAGE

There's a package
from my dad
on my bed.
I let it sit all day.
Megan comes over.
She picks up the package.
She shakes it.
"Aren't you going to
open it?" she asks.
"No."
"Ever?"
I shrug.
"Can I open it?"
"I don't care."

Megan tears off
the brown paper.
She lifts the lid
off the box.
She puts on her
little-devil grin
and plays
hide-the-gift-from-Bindi
for a minute.
Then she whirls around
and waves it
in my face: "Tah-dah!"
It's a sock monkey.

DUMPED

When we were moving
I dumped Ketchup,
my old sock monkey,
into the Goodwill box.
Mom must have told Dad.
(If they're so separated
why do they still

talk about stuff,
especially *my* stuff?)

"If you don't want it,"
says Megan, "I'll take it."
She cuddles it. "I think
it's cute."

I snatch it from her
and boot it under the bed
with the dust balls.

TWO A.M.

It's two a.m. by my alarm clock.
I've been jolted awake by a dream.
Dad was walking in the park
with a little girl. Holding her hand.
But she wasn't me.
He was calling her Bindi-boop.
I'm awake now and I'm crying.
Mom would hold me if I woke her,
but she went to bed with a headache.

I don't want to bother her.
I get up. On my hands and knees
I fish out the sock monkey,
brush dust balls from his tail.
I hug him. Tight-tight.
"Don't cry, Dusty," I tell him.
"Everything will be okay."
Right?

CAR

Ruby Frances
has put a down payment
on a used car.
Sky blue.
Shiny hubcaps.
One broken taillight.
Her next-door neighbor
is selling it.
Her grandmother helped
pay for some of it.
Ruby's tips will
pay the rest.

All she needs to
take it home
is fifty dollars more.
Uncle Tim
advises Ruby Frances
against buying
a junker.
But Ruby Frances
has sky-blue-car stars
in her eyes.

STARS OF MY OWN

I'm all starry-eyed
over Noah Adams.
His eyes are green.
I like watching him shoot baskets.
I like the way the ball bounces
my way at the park and how
I have to bounce it back to him.
I like how he half-smiles at me
sometimes. And how once
he asked me about the book
lying beside me on the bench.

"It's *To Kill a Mockingbird*," I told him.
He gave me a look.
"You into hunting birds?" he asked,
and went dribbling away.

REASON

When Albert finds out
I have a crush on Noah Adams,
he says he is disappointed in me.
"I thought you had better taste,"
he sniffs.
"What's wrong with Noah Adams?"
"Nothing, he's perfect, according to Noah
    Adams.
Just tell me this: How can someone who
loves books
like some dummy who thinks
To Kill a Mockingbird
is about hunting birds?"
"Well, I . . .
You see, he's just . . .
You don't . . ."
Hmmm . . .

So what if Noah
doesn't know about books.
In *To Kill a Mockingbird*
Atticus Finch says
you never understand a person
until you consider things
from his point of view.
I think from Noah's point of view,
basketball is more important
than reading.
The next time I'm at
Burke's Book Store,
I'm getting a book
about basketball.
So there!

BACON

Mrs. Otis, the Jingle Lady,
is driving us all nuts.
Complains.
Complains.

Complains.
Ruby Frances calls her Mrs. Picky.
(And worse.)
Today she scolds
Ruby Frances
for chattering too long
at Grace's table.
"I'm a paying customer,"
she calls out,
"and I have a complaint."
Mom goes right over.
"Grace pays, too, Mrs. Otis.
But please do tell me—
what seems to be
the problem?"
Mrs. Otis pokes at
her bacon
with a fork.
"I asked for crisp bacon.
You call this crisp?
See how it bends."
"The nerve of it,"
says Mom.
Mom picks up
the bacon,

holds it
in front of her like
a baby's wet diaper,
and marches
to the kitchen.
"Darnell," she declares,
"it seems like we must solve
the Case of the Bending Bacon, pronto!"
"Don't worry," says Aunt Darnell.
"She'll be able to chip a tooth
on the next batch."

STUPID RAIN

1.

I'm sitting in the back booth
trying to ignore
the thundering rainstorm
outside.
I sip hot chocolate
and read a book.
I come to the part
where Clara says to Heidi,
"Anger makes us all stupid."

I remember how mad I am
at my dad and I
slap the book shut.

2.
When I look up
I see Grace
at her usual place.
Her back is to me.
Her cart is, as usual,
right beside her.
Wig drenched,
flat against her head.
Light gray of her sweater
dark with rain.
Ratty red high-tops
and the wheels of her cart
in puddles.
Oh, Grace.

3.
I scurry back
behind the counter.
Do my little jobs.

Spray the front glass
of the pie case with Windex.
Wipe it spotless.
Flick a look at Grace.
A tiny voice inside my ear
whispers: *Do something.*
Another voice says:
Like what?
I mop up a spill of coffee.
Glance at Grace.
Do something.

4.

Homeless people
must be tough.
I refill the cracker basket.
Dart a look at Grace.
Do something.
It's none of my business.
It's grown-up stuff.
I'm just a kid.
Rinse the cake server.
Grace is getting up to leave.
She's pulling her cart,

sloshing and squeaking
across the floor.
She's reaching the door.

5.

"Stop!" I call out.
I race past Ruby Frances and
through the kitchen.
Past Aunt Darnell cracking eggs
and Thet spraying plates.
I go upstairs to our apartment,
grab an umbrella,
race back down.
Grace is gone.
I burst onto the sidewalk.
There she is—
two stores down,
slumping and slogging,
creaking through the rain.

6.

"Grace!" I call, and run to her.
"Grace—here!"
I push the umbrella at her.

Then I take it back. Open it.
Hold it over her head.
"Don't you need this, girlie?"
"No," I tell her. "We have
three other umbrellas, at least."
Grace takes the handle.
"Then I'll say thank you."
"You're welcome, Grace," I tell her.
And I run back to
my warm, dry home.

WHY?

Noah Adams has moved.
Away from here.
From me.
Why?
I can't believe it.
Megan and I were at the park.
The boys were playing basketball.
But not Noah.
I was too shy to ask about him.
So Megan did.

She marched right over.
"Is Noah around?"
"He moved," one of the boys said.
Moved?
One day he says "hey,"
and the next he's gone.
Why is *everybody*
leaving me?

COMMENTS

Ruby Frances tells me:
"You're overreacting. You
barely knew the guy."
But I *wanted* to know him.

Megan says: "It wasn't like
you were going steady."
But I would've if he'd asked.

Aunt Darnell says: "There's
plenty of other fish
in the sea, kiddo."
I liked *this* fish.

Uncle Tim says: "Aren't
you a little young
to have a boyfriend?"
No!

Mom says: "I know how
you feel, honey."
Does she?

Jackson says: "Stop
talking about this
lovey-barf stuff!"

JUST WHAT I NEED

Ruby Frances declares:
"I know just what you need, Bindi—
a shopping spree!"
She says every time she breaks up
with a guy
she buys herself
some new nail polish
or a bracelet
or a pair of shoes

or a toe ring.
She says it's impossible
to be totally sad
trying on toe rings.

AT THE MALL

Ruby Frances treats me to
a sparkly scrunchie for my hair.
Pink Mink lip gloss
and a fake gold toe ring.
I tell her, "You're using
all your car money on me."
"Not to worry," she says.
"I'll have that
fifty dollars
in no time."

DUMPED

When it comes to boy troubles,
shopping sprees seem to work better
for Ruby Frances than for me.

I like my new stuff—but I'm still
feeling sad. And dumped.

"You can't feel dumped if
you were never, um, picked up," says Megan.

"If I feel dumped," I tell her,
"I am dumped."
And in the dumps.

DARK

I'm in a dark mood.
My dark mood has hatched
one dark thought
after another.
I hope
Dad's peace lily will turn brown and die,
Noah Adams will hate his new neighborhood,
Mrs. Jingle Jangle Otis will grow a hairy wart on
    her nose.

These are rotten hopes.
I am not like this.

Mopey—okay, yes.
Mean and dark-hearted—never before.
I am scaring myself.
Me.

HELP

I need to talk to someone.
Fast.
I think about all the people
who care about me,
who will listen.

Mom
will worry too much.

Aunt Darnell
will feel she has to
tell Mom.

Uncle Tim
is always sweet to me,
but I'm afraid he will
just strut out another one
of his elephant jokes.

Ruby Frances
knows about boys
and makeup
and statistics,
but I doubt she's an expert
on dark moods.

Albert
is at the shore
with his dad this week.

Kyra
is still on her trip.

Megan
nearly fainted
over Witherspoon.
This mood of mine might
be too much for her.

Thet
is too shy.
And does not have enough English.

Mrs. Coleman?
Nope.

Dr. Bingo?
Uh-uh.

Who? Who?

I spot Grace
sitting on the old sofa,
fanning herself
with a newspaper.
Maybe . . .

JUST SITTING

I sit down with Grace.
She smiles at me.
At first we don't talk.
Just sit.
Together.
Looking down the alley
at traffic.
A bus burps by.
A yellow taxi
rattles past.
Grace fans us both

with the newspaper.
Something about
just sitting
feels calming.
Grace lifts my hand,
holds it to her cheek.
"You are a dear,
dear girlie," she says.

CONFESSION

I tell Grace
the truth.
I am not
dear
at
all.

GRACE SAYS

Grace listens as I go on
about my dark mood,
my mean wishes.
She tells me:
"If you were really mean
you'd be la-dee-dah-ing around
all smug and cold heart
and no worries
about feeling that way."
She holds my hand.
"Mean people don't confess,
or worry
about being mean."

ADVICE

Grace and I sit some more,
not talking.
Then Grace says:
"Sounds like things have been
rough lately, girlie.
Gotta ride it out. That's what I do.

And go easy on yourself."
I start to sniffle.
Grace turns. Lifts my chin.
Looks me in the eye.
"Life can be rough for
other people, too, y'know?"
I nod.
"Be gentle with other people, girlie."
I nod.
She's something.
Is Grace.

GENTLE

The next day
I water Dad's peace lily.
Gently.
Gently I thank Ruby Frances
for the shopping spree.
I hug Aunt Darnell.
I give Thet my biggest smile.
I invite Uncle Tim to tell me
one of his elephant jokes.
I gently slip an "I love you" note

into Mom's apron pocket.
And when Jackson slops
orange juice onto my shirt,
I tell him to
watch where he's going!
(But in my most gentle voice.)

A BETTER IDEA

Kyra is back from her trip!
I invite her to lunch.
She brings me a cowgirl mug
from Oklahoma
and a silvery seashell
from Virginia Beach.

Aunt Darnell
fixes us triple-decker
grilled cheese sandwiches.
Kyra and I make
our own root beer floats.

Jackson and his friend Cole
keep bothering us.

They blow straw papers
at us.
They poke us,
then run off squealing.
They call us poopy-heads.
I warn Jackson:
"I'm telling Aunt Darnell."
Jackson sticks his tongue out—
all show-offy in front of Cole.
"Wait," I say, "I have a better idea.
No more castle donations from me."

Suddenly Jackson wags his finger at Cole.
"You stop teasing Bindi and Kyra!
Right now!
Ya hear me?
Or *I'll* tell!"

BUZZ

Next day,
Jackson turns into
a little worker bee.
He scoots around
The Dancing Pancake,
dusting chair legs.
He crawls under tables,
flipping napkins
and fallen straws
into a trash bag.

He scoops up
two dead moths
and sprays Windex
on window bottoms.
He carries dirty spoons
to the kitchen.
"I'm working hard, Thet,"
he says.
He wipes a blob
of pancake batter
from Mom's shoe.

"I'm working harder
than you, Aunt Vera."

Tuesday:
A fifty-dollar bill goes missing
from the register.

Wednesday:
Ruby Frances pulls up to
The Dancing Pancake
in her sky-blue car. She toots the horn,
all excited. "Check it out, Bindi!"
she squeals. "Is this the most beautiful
thing you ever saw—or what?"

WHAT I THINK

I hate my brain when
I can't turn it off.
I don't want to think
what I'm thinking.

Fact:
Ruby Frances needed
exactly

fifty dollars
to buy the car.

Fact:
Exactly
fifty dollars
is missing
from the cash register.

Please
let me be
wrong about
what I'm thinking.

WHAT'S THE MATTER?

After The Dancing Pancake
closes,
Ruby Frances invites me
for a spin around the block
in her new car.
I tell her no thanks,
I'm busy.
She says, "It will

only take a minute."
I say, "I don't have
a minute."
She says, "What's the matter?"
I say, "Nothing."
She says, "Something's the matter."
I say, "You figure it out."
She gives me a look,
turns, and
drives away.

DILEMMA

Do I tell Mom
that I suspect
Ruby Frances
stole from us?

THE SCREAM

Mom is at the drugstore.
I'm still in my pajamas.
I'm brushing my teeth—and trying

to decide if I should tell Mom
about Ruby Frances—
when I hear a scream.
It's Jackson!
I drop my toothbrush,
race down the stairs.
Jackson is crouching under the table in a booth
clutching his milk carton bank.
Aunt Darnell is crawling on her hands
    and knees
trying to pull him out.
"Give me that bank!" she says.
"No!" screams Jackson.
"It's my money!"

Jackson confesses.
The missing fifty-dollar bill
is in his bank.
"But I didn't steal it," he wails
from under the booth.
"I worked for it.
Aunt Vera took money from
the cash register that time.
And I worked harder than Aunt Vera.
I worked harder than anybody!"

I'm too relieved it wasn't Ruby Frances
to be mad at Jackson.
And after all,
he did work hard!

MAD, MAD, MAD

But Ruby Frances
is mad,
mad,
mad

at me.
"How could you
think
I would steal,
Bindi?"
"I'm really sorry,"
I tell her.
And I so am.
But Ruby Frances
snarls at me,
"I so don't care
about your *sorries*."
She flounces
out the door.

CHEERY-CHERRY RED

Albert's back!
He calls.
"Want to paint your
slime-green room today?"
"Huh?"
"I have a whole gallon
of cheery-cherry-red paint,"

he says.
"Left over from painting
our kitchen."
I had been thinking
beachy-blue for my room,
but . . .
"Bring it over," I tell him.
"I could use some cheery."

SUGGESTIONS

Albert and I have
two walls painted.
We've been talking about
the situation with Ruby Frances.
"Just write her a nice note of apology,"
he suggests.
"She says she doesn't want my *sorries*,"
I tell him.
"That's because you only said it,"
he says. "Writing counts more."
"That's it?" I say.
"No. Buy her something. A gift."
"With my own money?"

"Definitely. And offer to wash her car."
I groan. "Anything else?"
He thinks. "Nope. Those should
do the trick."

NO TRICKS

The next morning
I give Ruby Frances
a handwritten note
of apology.
She reads it in front of me.
In front of me
she crumples it up
and tosses it into
the trash.

That afternoon
I use half my allowance
to buy Ruby Frances
a tube of
Wild Berry lipstick.
She gives it back.

"Not my color,"
she says.

I ask, "Would you
like me to wash your car?"
"No, thanks," she sniffs.
"I *always* keep it clean."
I have no more
tricks.

FORGIVENESS

This week's
Sunday school lesson
is about forgiveness.
I memorize all the main points.

HURT HUGGING

1.

It's Monday morning.
Ruby Frances is at the counter

eating French toast.
I ask if she's willing to listen to
what I learned at Sunday school.
She doesn't say no.

2.

I'm so nervous!
"Well, it's like, uh,
holding on to a hurt—
uh, hugging a hurt, one teacher
calls it. Well, it,
uh, like, just creates more hurt."
I breathe.
"That's it. That's what I learned."

3.

Ruby Frances pours
more syrup on her plate.
"That so?" she says.
I take another breath.
"Well, actually, there's more,"
I say. "Since God forgives us
for all the stupid,
thoughtless, mean things
we do and say,

we should forgive others."
I give her a long sideways look.
Is she listening?
"Right?" I say.
Ruby Frances just chomps away.
I plunge on: "If God never
forgave anyone, Heaven would be empty.
Right?"

4.
Ruby Frances finally stops chewing.
She seems to be speaking to
the syrup bottle.
"Are you talking about you and me?
Or about you and your father?"
What?

READY?

Lately I have been thinking
I may be ready
to start forgiving
my dad. I'm just not ready
to let anyone

know it.
I pull his picture
from my sock drawer.
I look at it
for a long time.
My dad.
Still . . .

GRACE'S CART

Someone stole Grace's cart.
"It was kids," she says.
She looks like she might cry.
Mom tells Officer Pike.
He says he will keep an eye out for it.
Uncle Tim brings Grace a blanket
from his car. And a handle bag to put it in.
"Just till you get your cart back," he says.
Ruby Frances seems to be over
being mad at me.
(She took me up on my offer
to wash her car.)
She pulls me aside, whispers: "Stolen stuff
is almost never found—statistics!"

BRIGHT IDEA

Ruby Frances and I
get a bright idea.
We will pool
some of our money
to buy Grace
a new shopping cart.
With a bicycle lock.

Albert says
his grandmother
will donate
one of her quilts.

Jackson pipes:
"Grace can have
my froggy umbrella."
I remind him:
"Your froggy umbrella
is ripped."
He dashes into the kitchen.
"Where's the 'duck' tape?"

Kyra offers a travel pillow.
Like new.
Megan offers brand-new socks.
Thet hands me five
one-dollar bills
from his wallet.
"For Grace-lady," he says.

Ruby Frances uses that
as an excuse
to throw her arms
around Thet.
"You are so generous!" she tells him.

Thet blushes.
But he doesn't
pull away.
Smart *and* nice.

Dr. Bingo has a summer cold.
When Aunt Darnell sends me over
with a jar of fresh-squeezed orange juice,
I see a sign in the front window
of his building
(well, Mrs. Coleman's building):
ROOM FOR RENT
A room.
Hmmmmmm.
A place away from mean kids.
A place to keep stuff safe.
A place out of the rain.
A place
for Grace.
Yes.

SURE OF IT

Mom and I can rent the room
for Grace.
I know money is tight,
but I can take less allowance.

And Mom has a good heart.
Mom will say yes.
I'm sure of it.

I tell Mrs. Coleman my idea.
"Can you hold the room?"
Mrs. Coleman is not so sure.
"Better talk it over with your mother
first," she says.
"Okay," I tell her. "But I know
what she's going to say."

WHAT MOM SAYS

"I'm afraid not, Bindi."
I am stunned.
"Why not?" I ask.
"Grace needs a room.
Mrs. Coleman has a room.
It's perfect."

"The room isn't free, Bindi.
It's for rent. Rent
costs money."

"I know that," I tell her.
"I can help. Just give me
less allowance."

Mom shakes her head.
"Even if you gave
all your allowance, honey . . ."

"What about Aunt Darnell?
Uncle Tim?
Maybe they would help pay.
We all have more
than Grace."

"But it's not just about the money."
"Then what?"
"The truth is, we simply don't know Grace
all that well."

WHAT'S TO KNOW?

I snap my fingers. "Hey—
no problem. I know Grace.
She was born in Oklahoma.

She reads the newspaper.
She likes toast with extra jam.
And pretty sunrises."

Mom takes my hand.
"Bindi, there's more
to know about a person."

"Like what?" I pull my hand away.
"That she's homeless? Is that what
you have against her?"
Mom says: "We don't know *why*
Grace is homeless."

"She's just poor," I say. "What other reason
could there be?"
"Alcohol, maybe," says Mom. "Drugs.
Problems.
We just don't know. We need to consider
Mrs. Coleman, too."
I stand up. "Mrs. Coleman said
it was up to you."
"I'm sorry, honey."

I hoped for my dad to come back.
Nope!
I hoped for Noah Adams to like me.
Double nope!
Then—unselfishly, I might add—
I hoped to rent a room for Grace.
Nope!
Anne of Green Gables said it best:
"My life is a perfect graveyard
of buried hopes."
Anne of Green Gables,
meet
Bindi of The Dancing Pancake,
a hoping dope.

JINGLE JANGLE

Mrs. Otis, the Jingle Lady,
says her table is full of crumbs,
says her grilled cheese
is rubbery,

says we forgot
her pickle,
says we don't know how
to run a restaurant.
Grace calls over:
"There's a diner
on Franklin Avenue.
Maybe you should
go there."
The Jingle Lady
calls to Grace:
"Maybe you should
mind your own business."
Grace says: "Maybe you
should stop complaining
so much?"
Mrs. Otis slaps money
on the table. (No tip!)
Stands up.
Walks out.
Slams the door.
"Yipes," says Ruby Frances.
"Uh-oh," says Aunt Darnell.
"Not good," says Mom.

"Brace yourself," says Uncle Tim.
"Mrs. Crabface!" says Jackson.

STAFF MEETING

The "Closed" sign is on the door.
Aunt Darnell takes a sip of coffee.
"Since we're just starting out," she says,
"we need every single nickel
if we're going to succeed."
Mom agrees. "We can't afford to
lose a single customer."
"I'll try harder," Ruby Frances promises.
Jackson pipes, "I'll be extra extra nice
to Mrs. Crabface."
"That's Mrs. *Otis* to you," says Aunt Darnell.
Uncle Tim says, "I'll have a little talk with
     Grace."
This bugs me. "What did Grace do besides
stand up for us?" I say.
Mom pats my hand. "She meant well, Bindi.
But sometimes meaning well
doesn't help."

WHAT IF? AND HOW COME?

Albert and I are sitting
on his back porch.
Albert is sorting through
his collection of bug photos.
I'm whining away like
the world can't hear enough of me.
Because I need to.
"What if my dad never comes home?
What if The Dancing Pancake fails?
And we have to move? *Again*.
How come I'm the only one who
wants to rent a room for Grace?

How come *my life* is such a mess?
How come you and Kyra and Megan
are always happy?"
Albert looks up from a photo of
the bark beetle.
"Did you say something?"

ALBERT'S TURN

I take a deep breath
and run it all by Bug Boy
again—minus the whine.
He listens. Doesn't sneak one
peek at a bug.
Then he does the talking.
He tells me he's sorry about
my dad.
He reminds me that my mom
is hurting, too. Just as much.
Maybe even more.
He says she's probably worried—
about the pancake business
and maybe having to move again.
He says if I can't rent a room

for Grace, maybe I can check out
a shelter for her.
He says he does have problems.
"And so do Megan and Kyra."
I'm shocked. "They do?"

OTHER PEOPLE'S PROBLEMS

Albert tells me he is worried
about his grandmother.
She hasn't been feeling well.
She is going to the hospital for tests.
He tells me Megan's parents
are thinking about sending her
to the new private school.
Megan doesn't want to go.
She wants to stay at Hamilton,
where all her friends are.
And Kyra's favorite cousin
didn't invite Kyra to
her birthday sleepover.
"How come I didn't know
any of this?" I ask.
Albert shrugs.

"Come on," I say. "Tell me."
He looks at me. Looks away.
"Maybe because you're only paying attention
to yourself."

REMINDERS

That night in bed
I think about
what Albert said.
Of course he's right.
Other people do
have problems.
I know that.
I think about the day
when Grace told me
to be gentle.
And I was—
for a few days—
and it felt good.
If only I didn't forget
so easily.
I get an idea.
I hop out of bed.

I get paper and markers.
I make two sets of signs.
One says:
THINK ABOUT OTHERS
The other reminds me:
BE GENTLE
I tape one set on my mirror.
And stick the other
in my shoes.

MY DAD THE POET

Dad e-mails me a poem:
Roses are red,
Violets are blue.
Never forget
That I love you!
There was a time when
I would have sent back
a snippy reply.
Or no reply at all.

I'm a nicer me now.
A gentler one.

A me who thinks that
maybe Dad is worried
or sad
or confused.

I type:
Sugar is sweet,
Peppers are hot.
Thank you, Dad,
That means a lot.
And then
I hit
"Send."

SOMETHING FUN

After dinner Mom says,
"Let's leave the dishes in the sink.
Let's do something fun."
"Like what?" I ask.
Mom grins. "Let's play hairdresser.
We used to do that
when you were little. Remember?"
I do.

Mom and I would do each other's hair.
Silly styles with clips
and scrunchies,
feathers and bows.
"Really?" I ask.
"Yeah," says Mom. "Let's dig up
all the hair doodads we can find."

PLAYING HAIRDRESSER

The nice thing about
playing hairdresser—
unlike Scrabble
or a movie
or reading aloud together—
is you can talk.
As I'm braiding Mom's hair
with bright purple ribbon,
she tells me she is proud of me
for being so concerned
about Grace.
She says: "You teach me a lot
about kindness, Bindi."
Then she tells me she is happy

that I am back talking to Dad—
if only by e-mail.
She says: "You teach me a lot
about forgiveness, Bindi."
I add two plastic roses
to the bottom of Mom's braids.
And a big gold clip
on the top of her head.
I hold the mirror up for her.
She bursts out laughing.
"And you teach me a lot about
being silly!"

I SHRIEK

My turn to be the client.
Mom begins brushing my hair.
She knows I like that.
It's soothing.
I relax in the chair.
I close my eyes.
Mom says: "I need to tell you
about some changes coming."
I jump up.
The brush falls to the floor.
My heart is pounding in my chest.

WHEN?

Mom pulls me over to the sofa
and onto her lap.
"Not all changes are bad, honey."
She smiles. "Dad found a job."
"That's the change?"
"One of the changes," she says.
I knew it—now the bad news.

"Okay, what else?"
"Dad's job is in this area."
I want to cheer. "He's moving back?"
"Back to the area, yes."
"Back to us?"
"Not exactly. He's moving in with
Aunt Darnell and Uncle Tim. For
the time being."
"Aunt Darnell?" I squeal. "She hates Dad!"
"Darnell doesn't hate your dad. She was
just mad at him for leaving us.
Is mad still."
"Why there? Why not here?"
"Because they're family,
and Dad and I still have some issues
to work through."
"So, work through them here!" I tell her.
Parents can make things so complicated.
She smiles, jiggles my earlobe.
"And risk putting you through a second
    separation?"
She shakes her head. "No way."
I jump up. "So, when is he coming? When do
I get to see him?"
Another earlobe jiggle. "Tomorrow."

THE PLAN

The plan is
for Dad and me
to meet tomorrow
in the park.
Just the two of us.
I lie awake
half the night.
What will Dad say?
What will I say?
Will we hug?
Will we cry?
Will it be awful?
And . . .
what will I wear?

GETTING READY

I wake up before the alarm.
Take a shower.
Wash my hair.
What to wear?
I pull stuff out of the closet.

Red T-shirt and white shorts?
Too casual.
Orange blouse and jeans?
Too autumny.
Shiny green skirt?
Too fancy.
Yellow polka-dot dress?
Yep.
Blue sandals?
No.
White sneakers?
Uh-huh.
I pull my hair back
into a ponytail,
the way Dad likes it.

Mom asks what I want
for breakfast.
Breakfast?
Is she kidding?
My stomach's already
full—
of butterflies.
"Just a couple bites of toast, then."
Okay. *Crunch. Crunch.*
"Good girl."

Mom goes down
to start the coffeemaker.
I change my shoes.
The blue sandals now.
I change my dress.
The daisy sundress now.
The butterflies are flapping
like crazy now.
Heart racing.
It's time.
Now.
Now!

FINALLY

I come downstairs.
Aunt Darnell looks up
from the grill.
"You look beautiful,"
she says.
"Doesn't she, Thet?"
Thet smiles.
Mom gives me a hug
and I'm off to the park.

The sky is blue.
The air is lemony-warm.
I see him. My dad. Standing near
the Cupid fountain.
I am a bird
in a flowered sundress
flying
finally
into my father's arms.

CATCHING UP

Dad and I sit on a bench
in the shade.
He holds my hand.
He asks me what I'm reading now.
I tell him: *"Pollyanna."*
I ask him what his new job is like.
He tells me: "It's a lot like my old job—
personnel manager."
He asks me how I like living
above The Dancing Pancake.
I tell him: "I'm kind of used to it now."
I ask him how he likes living with

Aunt Darnell and Uncle Tim and Jackson.
He winces. "It'll take some getting used to."
Finally I ask the Big Question:
"Dad, why did you leave us?"
He scowls, groans. "You're too young
to really understand, Bindi."
I give him what Mom calls one of my looks.
"C'mon, Dad. I deserve to know this."

ANOTHER ANSWER

"Okay," says Dad. "How's this?
You know I lost my job and was out of work
for quite a while."
"Yep."
"Well, that was hard for me."
"You were worried about paying the bills?"
"Not just that. Sad, too. Missing my work.
My colleagues. My routine.
Who I thought I was."
"So?"
"So, I got frustrated. Angry."
"At us?"
"Mostly at life, I guess. But

it spilled over into the way I acted with
your mom."

"Mad-sad-blue?"

"Yeah, well, and kinda disconnected.
Focused on myself too much. And *my* feelings.
Me. Me. Me. Not enough about her. Or you."
I think about what Albert said—
about only paying attention to myself.

"I understand," I say.

"Anyway, eventually I just got tired of failing.
Failing to find a job. Failing to make your mom
    happy."

"So you left."

"I thought if I got away it would be easier."

"Was it?"

"Yeah," Dad says.
He chuckles. "For a day or two."

"Dad . . . ," I say, then just stare at him.
He tugs at my ponytail. "What?"

"I'm afraid to ask," I say.

"Hey," he says. "What's to be afraid of?"
And he makes his famous Frankenstein face.
I laugh out loud.
Then he starts tickling me.
I scream. I squirm, beg: "Stop! Stop!"

"Are you still afraid?"
"No! No! I'll ask! Stop!"
He stops. He waits while I catch my breath.
"Okay," I say. I look at him.
"Dad . . . didn't you miss us?"
He doesn't speak the answer.
Maybe he can't.
But it's okay because the answer
comes another way—
in the best squeeze anyone has ever given me
and the tears that fall
from his eyes.

INTRODUCTIONS

Dad and I start walking back.
I point out Mrs. Coleman's building.
There in Dr. Bingo's front window
is Witherspoon, the skeleton.
Dad's eyes go wide.
"Wave hi," I tell him.
I take him to The Dancing Pancake.
I introduce him around.
"This is Grace," I say.

Dad bows. "Nice to meet you, Grace."
Grace smiles. "The pleasure is mine."
I explain to Dad that Thet doesn't
speak much English.
But Dad understands what Thet
is trying to say when he comes out with:
"Happy for this meeting, mister-sir."
Ruby Frances says, "Hi, Mr. Winkler."
While Dad is talking to Mom, Ruby gives me
   these big winks.
She whispers: "Some statistics can be wrong."
I look over at Mom.
She's laughing at something Dad said.
Now she's glowing.

HAPPY NEWS

Mom tells me:
"We can rent the room for Grace."
I squeal. I hop up and down.
I dance Mom around the living room.
"Really?"
"Yes. Really. You can thank Mrs. Coleman.
She cut the rent in half."
"I will. I'll go over there right now."
"And you can thank your father.
He's going to pay for it."
My dad!

HELPING GRACE

Everyone wants to help.
Albert's grandmother
donates a set of towels
for Grace.
Megan's parents buy Grace
two nightgowns and a robe.
Kyra brings
lavender soap and lotion

and a big bottle of shampoo.

We are all so excited.
Grace herself
seems a little quiet.
I'll bet she's so happy
she's speechless.

MOVING GRACE IN

Dad, Uncle Tim, and Thet
carry boxes.
Ruby Frances fluffs pillows.
I lay an afghan across the chair.
Mrs. Coleman brings fresh flowers
in a vase for the bureau.
Dr. Bingo presents Grace with an alarm clock
in the shape of a duck.
Mom hangs three pretty cotton dresses
in the closet,
alongside Grace's new robe.
Aunt Darnell slips underwear,
socks, and nighties
into drawers.
Jackson jumps up and down on Grace's bed.

"See how bouncy it is," he says to Grace.
Behind her cracked glasses
her eyes follow him
up and down.
She looks . . .
Hey!
What is that look?

HONEYSUCKLE, MOON, STARS

When Grace's room is ready,
Dr. Bingo shakes Grace's hand.
"Good night, neighbor," he says,
then heads across the hall

to his apartment.
Mrs. Coleman leaves next.
She tells Grace to let her know
if she needs anything.
The rest of us wish Grace
sweet dreams in her new home.
We start down the stairs.
Grace follows.
"That's your room, Grace," I tell her.
"Your bed. All nice and cozy and safe."
Grace nods. "I know. I just want to see
the moon. The stars. Hey—I think I smell
honeysuckle. Must be some on a fence
nearby."
"But that's your room," I say.
Grace puts her arm around my shoulder.
"I know, girlie. I'll go up in a few minutes."
Ruby Frances leads Grace back up the stairs.
She pipes: "Have I got a moon for you!"
She tugs Grace over to the window in
her room. She raises the shade,
points dramatically. "Here's your moon!"
Grace touches the windowpane,
says shyly, "I do like to smell the honeysuckle."
Ruby Frances throws open the window,

thrusts her head out, breathes dramatically.
"Mmm—honeysuckle!
Right here
in your
very own
room."

THE SOFA

I look out the back door.
A truck—"Big Red's Hauling Service"—
has clunked to a stop in the alley.
Two men hop out.
They lift the squashy green sofa—
Grace's sofa!
I run toward them. "Stop!" I yell.
Then I remember:
Grace has her own room now.
A real room.
Who needs that lumpy old sofa?
"Never mind," I tell the men,
who are looking at me as though
I have three heads.
"I mean,

get that old thing
outta here."

MORE ON THE JINGLE LADY

For someone who has only complaints
about us,
Mrs. Otis sure comes in a lot.
"I think I'll take my life
in my hands and try
the creamed chipped beef,"
she says.
"Hot. Not lukewarm.
I only hope I'll be able to find
some beef in the cream.
And wheat toast, not burnt,
like usual."

Ruby Frances gives the Jingle Lady
a big smile. She bows.
"Your wish is my command."

NOW WHAT?

"EEEEEEEEEK!"
What? What?
Has she seen a cockroach?
A ghost?
Why is she scattering
the silverware?
Why is she hopping around
like Jackson
when he's all sugared up?
Is the building on fire?
Why is Mrs. Otis screaming
her head off?

NOT A COCKROACH

It's not a cockroach.
Or a ghost.
Or a fire.

It's Inky,
Jackson's spider,
who somehow

made his way
back into The Dancing Pancake
and onto Mrs. Otis's plate of
creamed chipped beef.

TROUBLE

"It's fake," says
Ruby Frances,
bravely holding Inky
by one creamy leg.

"He won't bite you, Mrs. Otis,"
says Jackson.

Mom rushes over
to the table.
"I'll fix you
another plate
right away."

The Jingle Lady
is still twitching
and jangling

and puffing.
She wags her finger
at each of us.
She says: "No!"
Snarls: "You are all
in big trouble now!
I'm calling my son, Toby.
He's a big lawyer.
He'll inform
the Board of Health
about this revolting incident.
It'll be in every newspaper.
You can kiss this dump
goodbye!"
Yipes.
Uh-oh.
Not good.
What's next?

AFTERWARD

Aunt Darnell marches Jackson
back to the kitchen.
Jackson sniffles. "Inky

climbed out of my pocket."
Aunt Darnell scolds,
"Inky had no business
in your pocket
in the first place.
I told you before—
no Inky in the restaurant!"

When Jackson starts wailing
Mom picks him up.
"C'mon, little man, you're going to scare off
the rest of our customers.
Come upstairs with Aunt Vera."
Ruby Frances says, "I hope
that Mrs. Otis does go
to the newspapers.
It'll be free publicity.
Some movie star said that
bad publicity is better
than no publicity at all."

All the commotion
seems to have
confused Thet.
He looks at me, gestures

like *What's going on?*
"Not to worry," I tell him.
I pat his arm.
"The spider wasn't real
and my dad is back."
Why I said that
in this situation, I don't know.

Maybe because
I figure that Thet wouldn't
understand what I just said.
But he understands my smile.
He gives me a thumbs-up
and turns back to his dishes.
Thanks, Thet.

VISITING GRACE

I knock at Grace's door.
She calls: "Door's unlocked.
Come in."
She's sitting by the window.
She turns to me and smiles.
"Hi, girlie."

I say, "I brought you
an oatmeal cookie."
"That cop find my cart?"
she asks.
"No. Sorry," I tell her.
"But now you have a room
to keep your things safe."
"But I miss my cart."
I walk over to the window.
I change the subject. "Wow!
What a great view. You can
see everything that's going on."
"I had my stuff in my cart."
I sit on the arm of Grace's chair.
I pat her hand. "I know you did,"
I say. "But look at all
the nice stuff you have here."
"Is that cop really looking?"
Why is Grace all worried
about a rickety old cart when
she has this wonderful, clean room?
I change the subject again.
"Well, here's your cookie."
Grace takes it but
she doesn't eat it.

She folds it into a piece of cloth
from her pocket.
Then she tucks it
under the chair cushion.
"To keep it safe for later," she says.

LIKE WE PLANNED

Back at The Dancing Pancake,
Ruby Frances is getting ready to leave
for the day.
I tell her about my visit
with Grace.
"She still misses her cart."
"But Grace doesn't need a cart,"
says Ruby Frances. "She's got
a room now."
"That's what I told her," I say. "But
all she wanted to talk about
was that old cart."
Ruby Frances dumps her tips
into her purse. "That's weird."
I say, "Maybe we should still
go together and buy a cart

for her, like we planned."
Ruby Frances thinks about it,
nods. "Maybe this change
is a shock to her. Maybe
she needs something
from her old way of life."

CART-HAPPY

The next day, after Ruby Frances's shift,
we go to the hardware store
and buy a cart.
We drag it up to Grace's room.
When Grace sees it
her face goes all crinkly
like she's going to cry.
But then she laughs, grabs the cart handle,
and dances the cart around the room—
twirling,
swirling,
laughing.
A happy-dance
for a cart?
Go figure.

As we leave, Ruby Frances and I
slap hands. "I guess we were right
about the cart," she says.
"Yeah," I say. "Now our Grace
is finally happy."

SO FAR

So far no one from the Board of Health
is banging on our door.
So far, no letter from Mrs. Otis's son, the lawyer,
is slipping through the mail slot.
No front-page headlines in
the local paper.
No Mrs. Otis, either.
No "This egg is too runny.
This oatmeal's too lumpy.
This ham is too salty."
So far.

Maybe Inky
did us a favor?

GREAT

Megan is spending the night.
Earlier, Dad took us
for slushies.
Then to the hardware store—
the same one where
Ruby Frances and I
bought Grace's cart.
It's Dad's version of Heaven.

Dad got himself
a set of wrenches and
a new hammer.

He got me and Megan
each a flashlight.
Red for Megan.
Mine is black with a silver stripe.

Now Megan and I are in my room,
flicking our flashlights on and off,
giggling,
whispering,
making shadow puppets.

It's past midnight.
Megan says it looks like my parents
may be getting back together.
I tell her what Mom told me.
"Nothing is certain yet. We're
taking things day by day."

"Your mom seems happier, though,"
says Megan.
"I think she is, too," I say.
Megan taps my hand. "You
seem happier, too, Bindi."
"I'll tell you this," I say. "I'm happy you
don't have to go to the new school."
"Yeah—I finally convinced my folks."

I set my flashlight down
and flop back on my pillow.
"Funny, isn't it, how things
have just figured themselves out?
Everything seems to be going so great now."
"Yeah," says Megan, yawning. "It's all good."
Finally.

GONE

Grace is missing.
Mrs. Coleman says she hasn't
seen her in two days,
so she checked the room.
A few things were strewn around.
The vase lay broken on the floor.
Grace's clothes are gone.
And the clock Dr. Bingo gave her.
And the afghan.
And the cart.
Mrs. Coleman says she sat up
all last night in Grace's chair,
dozing off now and again.
But Grace never came in.
Dad says he'll drive around town
looking for her.
Mom says she'll contact Officer Pike.
I go to pick up the broken vase.
Ruby Frances yells: "Stop, Bindi!
This might be a crime scene."

TEAMWORK

Albert and I go looking for Grace.
We check the back alley for clues.
We ask around at the park:
"Anybody seen a lady in a curly brown wig?
Wearing glasses? Pulling a cart?"
"I should have taken a photo of her," I say.
"Then we could put up 'Missing Person' signs."
"Yeah," says Albert. "Offer a reward for
    information."
I get an idea. "Kyra likes to draw. She's good
    at it.
Maybe she can draw a picture of Grace for us."
"Good thinking," says Albert.

WHERE?

Kyra draws a picture
of Grace.
It looks pretty good.
Megan scans it
and prints out copies
on her parents' computer.

Kyra and Megan
and Albert and I
pass the pictures out
in shops,
at the supermarket,
in the park.
And, of course,
in The Dancing Pancake.
Where can Grace be?
Is she hurt?
Is she scared?
Is she lost?
Now it's starting
to rain.
Oh, Grace!

HIS TREAT

Albert feels like celebrating—
his grandmother's test
came back fine.
"Let's go to the movies,"
he says. "My treat."
"What's playing?" I ask.
"Night of the Tarantula,"
he tells me.

Because of Grace
I don't feel much like
celebrating.
And I sure don't feel like
seeing *Night of the Tarantula*.
But I've learned something
this summer:
It's not always about me.
So,
a dark room,
with screen-sized spiders?
"Let's go!"

SCHOOL SHOPPING

It's almost the end of August.
Swimsuits dangle from sale racks.
Beach towels lie in tangled heaps
on back tables.
Everyone seems to be
looking ahead to fall.

Dad takes me school shopping.
I've always loved
shopping for school stuff—
the bright candy-colors
of new folders,
the sturdy feel of fresh notebooks,
the smell of Pink Pearl erasers,
the pitter of paper clips
when I shake the box.

This time, though,
the fun of fall shopping
has the shadow of Grace
following me
up every aisle.

PRESCHOOL

In September Jackson will be
starting preschool.
Three days a week.
He's so excited, you'd think
he was going
to Disney World.

Jackson has given up
saving for a castle.
"It's taking too long," he says.
Now he's buying himself
stuff for preschool:
Spider-Man backpack,
big box of crayons,
drawing pad,
kiddie scissors.

He wiggles his little hips
and says, singsongy,
"I bet I get more homework
than you, Bindi."
Here's hoping
he's right!

Uncle Tim rushes into
The Dancing Pancake.
"I was just talking to Officer Pike—
they found Grace!"
Ruby Frances grabs Uncle Tim's arm.
"Is she dead?"
Mom swats at Ruby Frances
with a dish towel. "What a thing to say!
Grace is not dead"—
she looks at Uncle Tim, grabs my arm—
"is she?"

RELIEVED

Grace isn't dead.
Or hurt.
She was found over
in the next town, Ridgeway.
Officer Pike told Uncle Tim,
"The Ridgeway police say
she looks fine."

GRACE

So Grace is not dead,
but still there's plenty to
talk about.
Mom and Dad and I
are in the kitchen of our apartment.
Mom pats my hand
from across the table. "It seems
Grace wasn't happy in that room, honey."
"Who said?"
Dad gives me a crooked smile. "Grace said."
"You talked to her?"
"Yes," Dad tells me.
"I don't understand," I say. "Homeless people,
they need homes. They need to be off
    the street.
It isn't safe."
"Generally that's true," Mom says. "But Grace
is more than homeless people, Bindi. Grace
is Grace. She seems to need to be outdoors
most of the time. Being inside for long
seems to make her nervous."
"But why?" I ask.
Dad comes over to my chair,

puts his arms around me. "I don't know,
Bindi-boop. I don't even think Grace knows."
"So why did she go to Ridgeway?
Why not stay around here? Like before?"
Dad says, "Grace told me she was afraid
we'd be disappointed in her. That we wouldn't
want to be her friends anymore."

DISAPPOINTED

The truth is,
I am kind of mad at Grace.
Everyone worked so hard

to get her room ready,
to make things
nice for her.

I remember seeing
a family on TV once—
they had been homeless,
living in their car
near railroad tracks.

A group of firefighters
got together
and rented a house
for the family.
They gave them clothes
and toys,
food and furniture.
And the people were
so grateful.
They just beamed
into the TV camera.

Months later,
I saw the follow-up story.
The parents had jobs.

The kids were doing
great in school.
The family invited
the firefighters over
for a backyard picnic.
It was all so nice
and normal
and happily-ever-after.

Why couldn't Grace be like
that TV family?

LIFE

Kyra and I are sleeping over
at Megan's.
In her dusty-rose room
a pesky fly and the air conditioner
are buzzing away.
We're slurping ice pops
and talking about life
and how some things are
so hard to understand.
Like Grace preferring outside to inside.

Like Kyra's cousin not inviting her
to the sleepover that time,
then acting all nice at a family cookout,
as though she had not broken Kyra's heart.
Megan sniffs. "And what about Dr. Bingo—
lying about being a real doctor. If we did that,
we'd get in trouble."

We talk about Mom and Dad
and why they are dragging things out.
"If it were up to me," I say, "Dad
would have moved back in already."

Kyra swats at the fly. "You know what
I wonder about? Why some people are so icky—

like that Mrs. Otis?"
"Yeah," says Megan. "And why spinach
    has to be
better for you than French fries."
I throw my hands up. "And why God made
    sharks!"
"And blisters!" says Kyra.
"And flies!" says Megan.

"Life," sighs Megan.
"Life," moans Kyra.
"Flies provide food
for tons of birds," I say.
The girls stare at me.
"Albert," I say.

PUBLICIT-ICKY

The Dancing Pancake
makes the local newspaper.
Not in a good way, but
in a letter to the editor.

Dear Editor,
I'm writing to warn your readers
about the new cafe on Two Street
called The Dancing Pancake.
Flabby bacon! Rude waitress!
Oddball customers!
Noisy little tot bumping into tables!
And a huge spider in my
creamed chipped beef!

Sincerely,
Mrs. Bertha T. Otis

RESPONSES

Ruby Frances's face is bright red.
"Rude! I was plenty nice to that old crab apple."

"What about me?" whines Jackson.
"I'm not a tot. I'm big. I'm practically
in school. And I never
bumped into her poopy table."

Mom pulls her apron from the hook

and ties it around her waist.
She sighs. "We're definitely going to
lose customers."

Dad tucks a wisp of Mom's hair
behind her ear. He grins. "Only the ones
who don't eat spiders."
Dad grins a lot these days.

"We have to do something," says Aunt Darnell.
"Maybe more free pancakes.
Balloons. Banners. Advertising."

"That won't be cheap," says Uncle Tim.
I take a deep breath. "Okay," I say,
"I'll do it."
Mom eyes me sideways. "Do what?"
"I'll wear that dumb pancake costume.
I'll stand outside every day for a week.
Like a total weirdo.
I'll smile. I'll wave. I'll call out,
'Get your delicious pancakes!' "

"Do a pancake dance, too, Bindi,"
says Jackson.

He demonstrates.
Wiggle-wiggle.
Hop-hop.
Spin three times.
Wiggle.
Clap.
Wiggle.

"Better not press our luck, kiddo,"
says Aunt Darnell.
"Dear niece,
I'll just say thanks, before
you change
your mind."

DAMAGE CONTROL

We are hustling after dark
in The Dancing Pancake.
Tomorrow is the
new re-reopening.

This night, Dad and Uncle Tim
are cleaning.

Buckets slosh. Brooms swish.
Aunt Darnell is mixing up
the dry ingredients for pancakes.
Ruby Frances and Thet
are blowing up balloons
together.
I think they like each other.
Mom hangs streamers.
Jackson draws squiggles on
sheets of paper.
According to him, they say:
"Don't believe the nasty Jingle Lady."
I'm walking around
in the pancake costume
trying to get used to the scratchy feel of it.
Dad grabs my hand. He dances me
around the counter.
Everyone laughs.

It's a good night.
I find myself actually feeling sorry
for Mrs. Crabface.

HELP WANTED

Someone is tapping on the window.
Mom calls out: "We're closed."
Then Jackson yells: "It's Grace!"
Ruby Frances opens the door.
Grace comes in. She sets her cart
off to the side.
"I read that crummy letter to the editor,"
she says. "How can I help?"

WHAT'S IMPORTANT

I shriek: "Grace!"
I rush out from behind the counter
and practically swallow her
in a hug.
I can feel her squirming,

pulling back, staring at me up and down.
"Who? What—?"
Jackson shrieks. "It's Bindi!
Bindi the Dancing Pancake!"
Ten smiles together
wouldn't add up to the one
Grace is beaming at me.
"Hi, girlie," she says.

GOOD NIGHT

Dad walks Mom and me
up to the apartment.
Just to say good night.
I go to my room.
I get into my pajamas,
then start into the kitchen.
I stop.
There, in the dim light
of moon-through-curtains,
Mom and Dad are standing
hugging each other.
Yes!
Just for tonight.
Day by day.

BEING A PANCAKE

At first I'm shy.
I stand close to the door.
I feel like a total goofball.
Why did I ever agree to do this?

Jackson tries to pour
syrup on me.
I run.
I squeal for Dad to protect
my golden brown outside
and yellow-felt butter pat.

A little girl comes up to me.
She tugs at my costume.
"What are you?" she asks.
"I'm a pancake."
The little girl giggles.
"Hi, Miss Pancake."
"Hi," I say, giving her
a tiny wave.
That wasn't so hard.

I start waving to every little kid.
Then to every grown-up.
I am standing at the curb
waving to traffic.
Honk!
Toot-toot!
I am waving both arms.
Honk! Toot-toot!
Honk! Toot-toot!
It's a kind of music.
Okay—why fight it?
Deep breath . . . go for it . . .
a bounce . . . a twirl . . .
I'm dancing!
Me!

Honk! Toot-toot!
Honk! Toot-toot!
Cars are slowing down.
Walkers are stopping,
watching, clapping.
And I'm dancing.
I'm a dancing pancake!

BIG DAY

We were afraid hardly
anyone would come.
Or that Mrs. Otis would
show up with
a bunch of snooty, prickly people
holding signs saying:
"THIS PLACE SERVES SPIDERS!"
Instead it's our best day ever!
Even with free pancakes
we make a profit.
Customers pay for coffee,
bacon, omelets, oatmeal,
pie, and extras.

Some want to meet
the "noisy little tot"
they'd read about in the paper.
They give Jackson high fives
and money for the gumball machine.

Mrs. Coleman brings
her entire knitting club.
Officer Pike brings his family—
triplet daughters—and invites
Dr. Bingo to sit with them.
Mike the mechanic and his buddies
take up the whole counter.

Cabdrivers stop in.
Truck drivers.
Ten ladies from the Red Hat Society,
and Grace—with four of her friends,
who help hand out balloons.

During the day things break.
There are spills and mistakes.
There always are.
A lot of people hadn't even read
the Jingle Lady's letter.

Some came as loyal
customers and friends.
Some because they saw
our tiny ad.
Some because of the
"Free Pancakes" sign.
And some because
they were curious about . . .
"that dancing pancake!"

PARTY

Albert invites me over.
I walk into his den.
It's all decorated.
There's a wrapped present
on the chair.
There's a fancy cake
on the table.
Jeez Louise, I say to myself,
I forgot my friend's birthday.

"I'm so—"
I start to apologize,
but Albert laughs.
"It's not my birthday,"
he says.
I'm confused.
"It's for *you*, Bindi."
"Me?" I say. "It's not
my birthday, either."
Albert leads me to the chair.
He hands me the present.
I open it.
It's one of those
plastic trophy things.
It says: "World's Best Sister."
I get all choked up.

"I'm really proud of you,"
says Albert.
"You are?"
"Totally. You came through
a really rough time, Bindi."
"Not always with flying colors,"

LAST SLEEPOVER OF THE SUMMER

Megan and Kyra and I
are sitting on my bed
in our almost-matching pajamas.
We're all set for school to start
in one week.
We've spent the day doing
our summer reading reports.
Megan did hers on *A Wrinkle in Time*.
Kyra, on *Stargirl*.
I did mine on *The Yearling*.
Now that Dad is back in my life,
I was able to finish that book.

Megan asks why my parents
are still not living together.
I tell her my mom is taking it slow.
She says it's better to allow things
to unfold than to force them.
I tell Megan and Kyra
I think my parents are
unfolding nicely,
just like the blossom
on our peace lily,
which I can see
shimmering
from the doorway
of my room.